Strange Fruit

Dear Reader:

As a publisher, when seasoned author Michelle Janine Robinson decided to approach such a controversial subject in her latest novel, *Strange Fruit*, I was delighted to see that my prolific slate of writers are still constantly writing outside of the traditional publishing box. Imagine a world that reverses the legality of interracial marriages in the United States. The type of impact that such a ridiculous action would have on our diverse nation where it is commonplace for people of various races to become involved, get married and have children. That is what *Strange Fruit* is about and it is an amazing book.

Traci and Bill meet as neighbors in the same apartment building. She is black and he is white. Nature takes its course and they fall in love, decide to spend their lives together, and have a beautiful daughter, Caitlin. Then the world is turned into complete chaos. No one is safe, people have to make survival choices, and no one and nothing is as it seems. Traci and Bill find themselves having to hide their love, having to barricade their daughter in the basement, and end up battling each other as much as they are battling the world outside their front door.

I do not want to give the book away because there are many twists and turns that will get readers riveted. Robinson has a keen observation of the world and is a master at tackling controversy with compassion, imagination, and fast-paced storytelling.

As always, thanks for supporting Michelle Janine Robinson and the authors that I publish under Strebor Books. We appreciate the love and we strive to bring you the best, most prolific authors who write outside of the box. You can contact me directly at zane@eroticanoir. com and find me on Twitter @planetzane and on Facebook at www. facebook.com/AuthorZane.

Blessings,

Zane

Zane
Publisher
Strebor Books International
www.simonandschuster.com/streborbooks

ZANE PRESENTS

Strange Fruit

A Novel

MICHELLE JANINE ROBINSON

STREBOR BOOKS

NEW YORK LONDON TORONTO SYDNEY

Strebor Books
P.O. Box 6505
Largo, MD 20792
http://www.streborbooks.com

ISBN 978-1-59309-453-9
ISBN 978-1-4516-9650-9 (ebook)
LCCN 2012951353

First Strebor Books trade paperback edition March 2013

Cover design: www.mariondesigns.com
Cover photograph: © Keith Saunders/Marion Designs

10 9 8 7 6 5 4 3 2 1

Manufactured in the United States of America

For information regarding special discounts for bulk purchases, please contact Simon & Schuster Special Sales at 1-866-506-1949 or business@simonandschuster.com

The Simon & Schuster Speakers Bureau can bring authors to your live event. For more information or to book an event, contact the Simon & Schuster Speakers Bureau at 1-866-248-3049 or visit our website at www.simonspeakers.com.

For Justin and Stefan
From the day you were born
I learned my most valuable life lesson:
Narcissism is highly overrated.

SLAVERY: *Submission to a dominating influence*

COMPLACENCY: *Self-satisfaction, especially when accompanied by un-awareness of actual dangers or deficiencies, submission to a dominating influence.*

ACKNOWLEDGMENTS

I, like so many other women, am a huge fan of romantic movies, or chick flicks, as many would call them. After many years of self-evaluation, countless films, life and love, I finally understand why I *adore* such films. To quote one of my favorite chick flick characters, *Carrie Bradshaw*: *"I am looking for love; real love, ridiculous, inconvenient, consuming, can't-live-without-each-other love."* That's me, and finally, I can live my life secure in the fact that I have no need to make any apologies for all the subtle (and not so subtle) little nuances that make me, me, including my thoughts on love. Thank you, Candace Bushnell, and all the other fabulous writers on this planet that bring *all* of our stories to life and somehow make us feel like we're not alone in our thoughts, hopes, dreams and fantasies. In addition, I would specifically like to thank those writers who are especially near and dear to me, Zane, Charmaine Roberts Parker, Shamara Ray and Nane Quartay. Thank you all for not only turning up the proverbial heat, but also for including me in a very elite club.

. We all have favorite films; you know the ones—those films that make you laugh out loud, cry in earnest or shake your head in wonderment. I love a good movie; curling up on the couch with my favorite blanket and being catapulted to a world of fantasy. One of my favorite movies, *Sex and The City* has been praised, ridiculed and often (in my opinion) misunderstood. Yet, when all is said and done, the 2008 *Sex and the City* movie's worldwide total gross revenue was $415,252,786. Not bad for a film starring all women. Therefore, I would like to pay homage to the superstar women in my life, with my all-time favorite Carrie Bradshaw quotes.

"Maybe our mistakes are what make our fate. Without them, what would shape our lives? Perhaps if we never veered off course, we wouldn't fall in love, or have babies, or be who we are. After all, seasons change. So do cities. People come into your life and people go. But it's comforting to know the ones you love are always in your heart. And if you're very lucky, a plane ride away." To Jacqui Charles—I feel like there should be a warning to all young women while they go about their lives in pursuit of fun, shoes and men, that after falling in love, getting married, having babies and moving on, it's that best girlfriend—the one that was always there through thick and thin, that you'll miss the most. So, Jacqui, after years of traveling the globe together, it's high time I paid a visit to Ohio.

"Miranda was a huge fan of the Yankees. I was a huge fan of being anywhere you could smoke and drink at two in the afternoon without judgment." To Tarra Taylor and Christina Williams—Thank you both for braving the balmy heat and even the frigid cold with me at Redemptions, just so I could eat and drink in the out-of-doors, without judgment.

"Whatever happened to aging gracefully? [Miranda] It got old." Marciala Remouns—You were there for so many of my firsts, and thanks to you, I got my *very* first apartment. I was a teenager and scared to death of living alone and low-and-behold, there was this wise, funny and caring woman who lived right upstairs; just one short landing from my first-floor apartment. You opened your heart…and your kitchen to me and for that I will be eternally grateful. Every time my kids and I eat shepherd's pie, I'll think of you.

"As we drive along this road called life, occasionally a gal will find herself a little lost. And when that happens, I guess she has to let go of the coulda, shoulda, woulda, buckle up and just keep going." To my family—My mother, Sylvia Payne; my aunt, Dorothy Tillery; and my cousins, Linda Tillery, Nicole Tillery, Cindy Tillery, Michelle Tillery and Tiffany Tillery. I'm listening, really I am. I may not seem like it all of the time, but I hear everything you say and your words of wisdom are a part of me. I will exhale, I will relax and I will let go of all those useless thoughts that bind productive thinking.

"When real people fall down in life, they get right back up and keep walking." Although the basis of these acknowledgments is mostly to honor the women in my life, I couldn't possibly acknowledge anything good that has happened in my life without mentioning my unbelievable sons. Each day I marvel at how great it is that I not only love my children, but I like them as well. To some this may seem a given and completely simplistic, but everyone who is reading this should try an experiment: hold anyone in your life up as an example—family member, spouse, child, that co-worker who you go to lunch with every day—and ask yourself this one question: If they were *not* a family member, a spouse, a child or a co-worker, would you still want to spend time with them? That is the difference between loving someone and liking someone. The two are *not* mutually exclusive. Justin and Stefan, always know that when no one else does, I get you. One of my favorite times of the week is Sunday nights at 9:00. What are we going to watch on television when there's no *Walking Dead*? If I know you, like I think I know you, you guys got the *Walking Dead* reference way at the beginning of this paragraph!

"One woman's pornographer is another woman's spiritual leader." *Carrie Bradshaw* said it first, but I, Michelle Janine Robinson (a.k.a, *The Black Carrie Bradshaw*) frequently echoes these words. After

all, isn't it grand to live in a world where all perspectives are available for our mental consumption? I may not like everything I read or watch, but I am appreciative of the multiplicity at my fingertips.

Thank you for picking up a copy of *Strange Fruit*. Enjoy!

Love,
Michelle Janine Robinson

PROLOGUE

*P*ractically barricaded inside of her own home, Traci Bianco looked apprehensively past the thick curtains and blinds, meant to camouflage her existence, through the barred windows and over the town she once loved. She wondered if New York would ever be returned to its former glory. She was not optimistic.

The Nation's post-cataclysmic existence had at least spared her the most insidious of fates-for now, but only because of whom she had married long before the devastation reached full tilt. Eventually, even that would not be enough to spare her. Desperation was commonplace and the level of atrocities continued to mount with each passing day, leaving ordinary people desperate and searching for answers.

While her daughter, Caitlin, played quietly in her bedroom, Traci retrieved a metal lockbox from beneath a floorboard in her closet. Inside the box were small remnants of what remained from her former life. She carefully removed a newspaper, weathered by age. The November 5, 2008 headline read, *"RACIAL BARRIER FALLS IN DECISIVE VICTORY."* Behind the iconic newspaper was another *New York Times*, dated November 7, 2012, which simply read, *"PRESIDENT'S NIGHT."* Her fingers caressed the front page lovingly.

It was difficult to imagine that so much could have changed in less than fifteen years. It was 2025; fourteen years after the 9/11 tragedy of the Twin Towers terrorist attack and only ten years after The Empire State Building was toppled by an explosion. Thousands of lives had been lost as a result of both terrorist attacks and the media's coverage had been vast and dramatic. By sharp contrast, slavery in America had been mostly ignored for years, except for a few organizations that attempted to warn the public of the fate of the world if modern-day slavery continued to be ignored. Women and children were trafficked into the U.S. from other countries for years, and forced into prostitution, while men served as slave labor and were kept in poor health and squalid living conditions. However, it was Hurricane Molly in 2018 and The Stock Market Crash of 2020 that had sealed the country's fate.

Traci kept glancing at the doorway, nervously, careful not to draw the attention of her husband or her daughter. Even the black blinds and curtains didn't seem to be enough. At only four years old, Caitlin was still young enough that she didn't quite understand the world she was living in and the rules that were actively enforced, nor did she understand how drastically the world had changed in such a short period of time. Yet, even the young were not protected from all awareness. Children like her daughter were dying every day, simply because of the color of their skin. Traci's husband, Bill, did, however, fully understand. He often cautioned Traci about her choices under the United States' current regime. Traci was angry and often dangerously willful; that is why she kept the lockbox and its contents, reminders of her former world. She was well aware of the fact that Bill could never know for many reasons, not the least of which was that his awareness of her *contraband* would mean that he was guilty of even more than marrying and concealing a black woman. His awareness of the items she was keeping would mean treason and he would therefore be subject to punishment by U.S. Law, including imprisonment or maybe even death. Despite the obvious strain placed on their marriage, she still loved Bill and she believed he loved her as well. And, even if neither of them loved one another enough to survive their current catastrophic state, she was sure that they *both* loved their daughter. Bill's survival was tantamount to any hopes for Caitlin's future safety.

"What you got there?"

"Nothing," Traci lied.

"You and I both know that's not the truth. You realize what would happen if that was found?"

"Yeah, I know; the same thing that will happen if I'm found. Who would have thought that one day I'd be a prisoner in my own home? I can't leave and I can't stay. Ironic, isn't it."

"It's only temporary. I'm making plans. We're going to get out. We're going to get out together."

Traci understood exactly what that meant. For months Bill had tried everything he could to get passports for Traci and Caitlin. When he realized that might not work, even if he did secure a passport, he realized he would have to find a way to escape from the U.S. with or without a passport. The question Traci kept asking him was where? The U.S. had not been the only country affected. For quite some time they believed the only alternative they had was to somehow make it to Germany, where her brother and sister-in-law were. Unfortunately, over time it had become apparent that even Germany was a dangerous gamble.

Bill observed the forlorn look on Traci's face and searched for the words to fill her with some small remnant of hope. "There has to be somewhere we can go. The entire world can't be affected by this madness. There's always been some other place, some small corner of the world to go to, even in light of the greatest despair."

The frightening and intrusive presence of what sounded like a battering ram pounding against their front door signaled the realization that, for Traci and Bill Bianco, time had run out.

CHAPTER ONE

"Hey, bro, did you vote?"

"Hell yeah, I voted! I hope everybody else got out there and cast theirs. You know how we do. Most of us talk a mean game, but when it comes to really showing out and making our voices heard, we leave it up to the next man."

Traci rolled her eyes.

"I saw that," Darren said.

"What?"

"You know what; that sister-girl eye roll thing you do. You've been doing it since we were kids. I can see it as clearly as if you were standing right here in front of me, even while I'm talking to you on the phone."

Traci laughed. "You know me way too well, brother dear. It's a reflex action. My eyes automatically go into 'roll mode' when I detect you're about to step up on your soapbox."

"Oh no, you didn't. You see what happens when a brother like me tries to drop some knowledge? Folks get all resistant to hearing the truth; even my own sister! Speaking of knowing you too well, please tell me you didn't vote Republican."

"You're not supposed to ask me who I voted for."

"Knowing you, it wouldn't surprise me in the least if you went all Republican on me. I fully understand your predilection toward vanilla flavor. Hell, I've enjoyed my own bit of jungle fever in the past. But, when it comes to politics, a black Republican ain't fucking natural. I mean, really, talk about a goddamned oxymoron. How can *any* black person be black and Republican at the same time, especially when the Democratic candidate is black?"

"I'm not going to go there with you, Darren. You and I both know that could take hours. However, I will say this. I voted for who I believed to be the best candidate, regardless of color. I hope that's what you did as well. Besides, my choice of men is irrelevant. I loved Bryan, a black man, with all I had and look where it got me. Don't get me wrong; his being black wasn't a factor. I've dated all kinds of men and I'm just saying, good and bad comes in all colors."

"I'm sorry you got hurt, sis. You didn't deserve that, but I'm not even going to sit here and lie. My first alliance is always going to be to my people. I wouldn't have cared if J.J. from *Good Times* was running for President. I would have voted for him. As a people we've endured slavery, unfair imprisonment and all manner of discrimination from A to Z. I owe it to every generation that follows me to elect a black man President, again, so that my children and your children and all the little black children that follow know that they can be anything they want to be, including President of these United States. There was a time when children couldn't believe that. Now they can. Hell, there was a time you and I couldn't even vote. With a second term, the message will be clear. It will prove that his election was not a fluke or something handed to him. It will prove that the people, both black and white, decided and democracy ruled. We *all* owe it to our children, including you, to ensure that we play this game called life on a level playing field. That means a black man has as much of a right to be President of these United States as any other man."

"Or woman," Traci chimed in.

"Or woman," Darren agreed. "In fact, if it were up to me, we'd be electing a black woman. That'd show 'em; one of ya'll as President of the United States. I get chills thinking about it."

"What exactly are you trying to say? Just remember, choose your words carefully since I happen to be one of those black women you're about to stereotype."

"Naw, naw, don't get me wrong. A black female President would be cool. I will tell you one thing though, every twenty-eight days the country would be fighting with somebody, somewhere and weave hair would be dirt cheap, everywhere."

"Darren Sanders, you're lucky you're on the phone and in Mississippi and not standing in front of me. If you were here I would kick your ass. You see how you do? If somebody was talking about a black man like that you would be ready to call the NAACP."

"Dear sister, I forget sometimes how much older you are than me. If I were making the call it would be to Color of Change. That group is on point. They are actively addressing the issues that confront a brother like me in this modern-day world we find ourselves living in."

"What are you, their spokesperson?"

"No, but I am considering becoming a member."

"Be careful, Darren, you being a teacher and all, especially in the South. You don't want any of your affiliations to jeopardize your career. You already have enough going on, without adding that to the mix."

"Don't worry, big sis. I'm good. I'll be smart and prudent in my approach to all things militant."

"Militant? Now whose age is showing? Do people even use the word militant anymore?"

"I don't know about people, but I do."

"Have you spoken to Mom lately? She called me a couple of weeks ago about a letter she got from her housing project. Apparently, those living in public housing are now required to work for their shelter, one way or another. They want them to clean up the grounds, mop the floors and stuff like that."

"What the fuck? I know damned well they didn't send *my* mother a letter asking her to do work around that cesspool. She did her time. She worked and retired and her rent is paid from her own pocket, not from government funding."

"I guess, *technically*, it is considered government funding, since it is public housing."

"That's some straight up bullshit!"

"I completely agree with you. I told her to send me the letter and that I would deal with it. I'm sure it's probably a form letter that is sent to everyone living in the complex. They can't possibly expect a seventy-seven-year-old retired woman, who is paying rent, to go out and clean up the building?"

"You're probably right, but I still think it's a bunch of bullshit. The majority of people forced to live in public housing are there because they're either unemployed or underemployed. Hell, instead of making folks clean the damned grounds and shit, they should be helping them to get real jobs with real pay. It's fucking slavery all over again!"

"Look who's talking about slavery, Mr. Darren Sanders. You were the last person I expected to pack up and move to Mississippi, of all places. That's like the belly of the beast. I half expect to find some slaves that were *never* freed still pining away for their freedom."

"Oh, stop it. It's not that bad here. The truth is, as quiet as it's kept, racism is alive and well in the North as well; always has been. Folks put a pretty bow on it there, *especially* where you are in New York City. Besides, I moved here for love."

"Don't remind me. You packed up your entire life to move to

Mississippi and that dick left you for someone else. I still can't believe you didn't come back after the two of you broke up."

"Baby girl, you know that's the African-American dream. All black folks wanna move back down South. Not only that, I feel like I'm needed here much more than I was in New York City."

"I need you."

"That's all well and good but I was talking about work. In New York I was constantly trying to stay one step ahead of the funding curve. No sooner did I feel like I was making an impact, whether it was HIV counseling or educating families, and suddenly the program would lose funding and I was on to the next program. It's different here and if I'm going to constantly live in fear of losing my job, at least I can do it in a place where the cost of living is a *lot* lower."

"Not all black folks. The last place I want to be is anywhere in the South. Hell, I don't even want to be in the North. This city is draining the hell out of me. If it were up to me I'd be living in Tuscany somewhere."

"I was half expecting you to say Germany."

"Believe me, I've considered it."

"I know you have. Our brother and his wife would love having you there. They'd probably throw a parade in your honor. Now me, on the other hand, that's another story altogether."

"What do you mean? Sebastian loves you, and so does Angelika."

"I have no doubt that they both love me. However, Sebastian has clearly never gotten used to the idea of his brother, the queer."

"Oh, Darren, don't say that."

"It's the truth. I make him uncomfortable."

"I guess it's just a guy thing," Traci offered.

"Yeah, it's a guy thing. In the meantime, I haven't seen my own brother in almost five years."

"The two of you are ridiculous. Do I have to do an intervention? Tell you what. I was planning on visiting for Christmas. Why don't we make it a family affair and spend Christmas in Germany?"

"You'd better check with Sebastian and Angelika before you make plans like that."

"It's no big deal. I already spoke with them months ago and mentioned I might come for the holidays. They do it up big for Christmas in Germany. Instead of one day they celebrate for several days. Anyway, Sebastian and Angelika are expecting me."

"The key word here, Traci, is they're expecting *you*, not me."

"So, we'll add one more person to the mix. Their house is big enough to hold us and if it's not, we'll stay in a hotel. If Mom weren't so terrified of flying, I would try to get her to come as well. I just know what the answer is going to be."

Darren chuckled. "You can forget that," he said.

"Yeah, I know. Anyway, Darren, I've got a lot of studying to do. Promise me you'll think about it and don't be such a stranger, okay?"

"I promise."

"You know I love you, right?" Traci asked.

"Of course I do. I love you too, Traci."

"Stay safe," Traci added.

"Always. Later."

After she hung up, Traci realized her comment about safety was more than general. She worried so much about him. Being a black gay man in the South couldn't be easy.

Glancing at the clock, Traci realized that she and Darren had been on the phone for almost two hours. She grabbed a quick bite to eat from the fridge, while looking through an old photo album with pictures of her and Darren when they were kids. Pleasant memories of her childhood lulled her to sleep. Unfortunately, those memories didn't sustain her through her dreams. Those were full of Bryan. As hard as she had tried, she still couldn't shake him, not even when she slept.

Some time around midnight, exhilarated voters shouting four more years awakened Traci from a sound sleep. The voices full of enthusiasm chanting outside her window were almost enough to help her forget her dreams, and Bryan. Despite the fact that she was embarking on what she hoped would be a great new start, she couldn't help but bemoan her former life. In that life she had been in love with the same man since she was a girl. She and Bryan had been dating since they were both in high school. After college they moved in together and she believed that they would eventually marry. That is, until she had arrived home early from work one day to discover the love of her life in bed with her best friend. There had been lots of tears, and even more yelling and screaming, before Traci slammed the door behind her, leaving Bryan and everything associated with that old life far behind her. She decided it was time for her to live the life she was intended to live and not Bryan's life or the life everyone else expected her to live. That meant trading the "burbs" for a place in the city and her nice safe job at the insurance company for school, once again. She had always wanted to teach but Bryan and her mother had convinced her it was mostly a thankless job and not very financially lucrative. Clearly, Bryan was no longer a consideration and her mother would have to understand that she was a grownup and therefore had to make her own life decisions.

When Traci moved, she took very few of her belongings with her. Somehow, everything seemed to remind her of Bryan. Instead, she convinced herself that it might be fun to start from scratch. That's what she was doing when she met Bill.

"You need some help with that?"

Traci turned to find an attractive man with penetrating grayish-green eyes and olive skin smiling broadly at her.

"Um, yeah, I could use a little help," she admitted.

He hoisted the large box onto his shoulders and, for the first time in a long time, Traci found herself attracted to someone other than Bryan. Despite the fact that he wasn't a large man, physically, his presence was one of great stature. He seemed to possess an air of strength and power from within, by which she was instantly intrigued.

"What floor?"

"Oh, yeah, I'm on the third floor; three A," she responded, distractedly.

"Three A it is!"

"Thank you so much. I was just taking a little rest."

"No problem. Besides, no woman as beautiful as you should be reduced to doing manual labor. Where is your husband, at work?"

"Don't have one of those."

The expression of pleasure emanated from his entire being.

"I guess that's all the more reason I should have paid for white glove delivery."

"No worries. Bill Bianco at your service."

As soon as he entered her apartment Traci was aware of how sparsely furnished her place was.

"Just moved in?" he asked.

"I've been here a couple of months. I don't have much furniture, but I do have coffee. Would you like some?"

"I would love some."

Traci was surprised at how easy it was to talk to Bill. It was as if she had known him for years. She knew she should probably put on the brakes on the runaway train in her head, but it all reminded her of one of her favorite films, *Cloud Atlas*. She somehow felt as though she had known him before, maybe in another lifetime.

These were the times when she got angry with Bryan and Jennifer all over again. She missed having a best girlfriend to bullshit with. She talked to Darren all the time but it was different with a really good girlfriend. Traci made a mental note to get out in the world and mix and mingle. That was what Darren told her; that she couldn't meet anyone, male or female, by sitting in the house, although her encounter today had proved a loophole in that statement.

She hoped her handsome neighbor wasn't married or living with someone. That seemed to be the other problem she had. Every time she met a man, he was already involved with someone else. What the hell was wrong with people anyway? Wasn't it hard enough spending time with one person at a time without making things extremely complicated? When she was dating some- one, she enjoyed focusing all of her attention on that one man. The thought of a steady influx of multiple men made her feel exhausted. She had enough to think about with work and her dreams for the future without trying to keep straight which man was which. Although she was willing to admit that was probably a woman's way of thinking. Men seemed to have no problem at all with juggling more than one woman at a time with ease. Or, maybe it wasn't with as much ease as it appeared.

Her ex, Bryan, apparently, not only enjoyed juggling, but couldn't control himself enough not to juggle with her best friend, or to do it with her in their bed. That's why she was here and he was there. Traci could tolerate many things, but displaced loyalty was not one of them. So, she had given Bryan, the love of her life, the boot. Or, technically, she had booted herself, since she was the one that moved out. She realized she would never have been able to stay in the apartment. Everything she looked at would have reminded her of him and, at some point, of her.

Traci was online cruising Facebook when she saw a friend request from her handsome neighbor. She was flattered. Obviously, she had made an impression. Traci was blown away by how quickly he had moved.

She hit the button to accept his request and hoped he wouldn't end up as yet another one of those *friends* on Facebook she never even talked to. Somehow, she didn't think that was the case.

As soon as she accepted his friend request, there was an IM from him.

"So, how do you like the new digs?"

"Getting used to it," she replied. "How long have you been in the building?"

"Not long. I was living in New Jersey and I decided it was high time I got out on my own."

"Same here."

"So, we're embarking on new territory. Isn't it exciting when you try new things?"

"Yes, it most certainly is."

"I'm glad this is the building you chose. It's great having nice new people in the building. See you around the building," he said.

"See you."

Traci had gotten the distinct impression that she was going to like it there.

After she logged out of Facebook, she got another IM Message. This time it was on Hotmail and it was from Bryan.

"I miss you."

She wasn't sure whether she should ignore him or verbally spar with him. She was still so mad. What he and Jennifer had done was unforgivable. There was no way she could talk to him without saying something she would feel ridiculous about later or, worse yet, something she would truly regret.

CHAPTER TWO

"Good morning."

Traci turned to find Bill walking right behind her. The two of them had settled into a comfortable, yet distant routine. There was the typical neighborly banter. To Traci's dismay, for months, that had been all. As much as she realized a rebound relationship was the last thing she needed, she had to admit to herself that she had been hopeful after their first meeting that there would have been more. Instead, it was little more than polite conversation.

"Good morning," she responded.

"You look very nice this morning. Got plans after school?"

"No. I've been interviewing for a better job, or maybe an additional job. As glamorous as it sounds, my work as a barista barely pays enough to keep a roof over my head."

"I didn't know you were job hunting. I'll keep my eyes and ears open. I might know some people that can help you out."

"Thanks, Bill. I appreciate that."

"No problem. Any way I can help. Good luck today."

"Thanks again. You have a good day."

"I will now," he replied.

After months of this, Traci wasn't sure whether she was misreading the signals, but that last comment, much like many others he had made through the months, sounded like very obvious flirting to her. She decided he was either already involved with someone else, gay, or both. As she left the building, she could feel his eyes boring a hole through her. His reflection in the glass door as they exited the building revealed much. The way he was looking at her made it crystal clear he was definitely not gay. She almost wished he were. At least that would explain why he hadn't made a move yet.

Once outside, Traci bundled herself up against the chilly morning air and focused her attention on getting to her first interview on time.

She couldn't believe that after hours of going from interview to interview she was still no closer to pinning down even the prospect of a job. Every place she went to it was something. Either she was under-qualified or over-qualified, too eager or not eager enough. It was so frustrating. Even with the aid of a headhunter, she was getting nowhere.

Traci decided to take a short break before going home to get ready for school and stopped into Starbucks for a cup of coffee. She was beginning to think both Bryan and her mother were right about her going back to school when she pulled out her Android and began looking through some of the postings on the many career sites she had been utilizing for her search.

A posting on Monster.com for a personal assistant to an entrepreneur caught her eye. If the information posted on the website was truthful and accurate, the position was perfect. It paid well, the hours were flexible and since the job was very much one-on-one, it afforded her the autonomy she was not likely to find working anyplace else.

She was right. The job was perfect and eventually Traci began to settle into some sense of normalcy. School was going great and in order to finish as quickly as possible, she doubled up on her class load. Then, as if out of the blue, she was sitting at home studying when she received an instant message on Facebook.

"How goes it?"

"I'm good. How are you?"

"I've been thinking about you."

"Yes!" Traci said rather loudly.

For a minute she almost forgot he was right downstairs and decided her joy at having him contact her should be confined to low whispers.

"Really?" she said.

"You seem surprised."

"A bit; I've been here almost a year and so far most of our conversations have consisted of talk about the weather and the building. The most personal thing we've talked about is my job search."

"Right you are. I guess I'm overly cautious."

"About what?" she asked.

"You know; the fact that we live in the same building and all. Also, it occurred to me that I might not be your *type*."

Traci wondered if he was talking about the fact that she was black and he was white, but decided not to attempt to find out.

"I don't have a type."

"In that case, is there any chance you'd like to have dinner with me?"

"Sounds like a plan."

"Great! You free this Friday?"

"As a matter of fact, I am."

"Friday it is."

"Friday," she confirmed.

"So, how's the new job?" he asked.

Traci chuckled.

"Are we back to that again?" she typed. "Next you'll be talking about the building and the weather."

"Don't worry. I'll never, ever talk to you about the building or the weather again. I do want to know about the job, though. In fact, I want to know all there is to know about you."

That was all Traci needed to hear. For so long she had a pattern of dating men who talked only about themselves and seemed to care less about what was important to her. It was nice to have a man say he wanted to know all about her. She hoped it wasn't pure hype. Although Traci realized she should probably be spending the time studying, she couldn't resist continuing the conversation they were having.

"You know this is ridiculous," Bill typed. "We've been instant messaging one another for a solid hour. We could be having dinner right now."

"That would be great, except I already ate."

"Yes, you may have eaten dinner, but I bet you haven't had dessert yet."

"Bill Bianco, I hope that wasn't some cheesy pickup line."

"No, Smarty Pants! Let's go get some dessert, really."

"I'm supposed to be studying, but if there's one thing you should know about me, it's that I *never* say no to dessert."

"I'll meet you downstairs in a half-hour."

"A half-hour it is."

Traci was happy he hadn't said now. She had her hair in two messy plaits and was wearing a ratty old pair of sweats and a wife beater. She quickly washed her face, combed out her beautifully layered hair, sparingly applied a bit of makeup, and eased her way into a pair of faux leather tights and a denim shirt. By the time she got downstairs, she was five minutes early and he was already there waiting.

Traci had never embraced the technology age with as much ardor as so many others. Yet, at this very moment she understood the appeal of technology and social networking more than any other time in her life. She was suddenly more nervous than she had ever been on *any* date. She believed it was because the ease at which they had been able to talk with one another while instant messaging was gone. Here they stood face to face. Sure, they were neighbors, but after spending an hour learning so much about each other, it suddenly dawned on her that for all intents and purposes, they were little more than convenient strangers.

"Hi," she said awkwardly.

"Hey, beautiful. Before we start talking about the weather again, I have to tell you where we're going. The name always makes me laugh. Something tells me we both need a little something to break the ice. Isn't technology such an intimacy set-up?"

She was overjoyed that he seemed to be thinking the same thing she was.

"Yeah, it sure is."

They both laughed.

"Well, clearly we don't need an ice-breaker any more, but I'll tell you the name of the place anyway. It's Momofuku Milk Bar."

Traci wasn't sure if the name really was that funny or if this was nervous laughter, but she was still laughing by the time they exited the building.

"The place is on Thirteenth and Second. You wanna walk it?"

"Yeah, I could use a walk."

Traci couldn't get over the fact that as nervous as she had felt only a few minutes earlier, she wanted him to touch her. She kept resisting the impulse to hold his hand or lace her arm into his. Just when she started to think that she was moving way too fast, at least in her head, he grabbed her hand as they crossed the street and held fast to her all the way to Momofuku's Milk Bar.

Anyone in their presence would have thought they had been drinking. They were in the grips of that incredible sense of intoxication that could only be derived from the early phases of a great romance. Hanging on one another's every word, the daring and flirtatious innuendoes and that overwhelming desire to see the other person naked.

As comfortable as they had been with one another all night, the walk back home was surprisingly quiet. Bill decided he would once again use humor to ease the tension.

"Let's take a cab. I'll drop you off first."

"Funny. You beat me to the punch. I was going to say your place or mine."

The comment was only out of her mouth a few seconds when she realized that what she had said sounded more like an invitation for him to come with her upstairs to her apartment than it was a joke about them living in the same building.

"I, uh...," she began.

"No worries, Kitten. I know what you meant."

His use of a pet name in addressing her was enough to melt her heart—among other things.

As much as she would have liked to invite him upstairs, Traci wanted that *new leaf* she was turning over to encompass all facets of her life, including the way she dated. So, instead of inviting him in under the premise of a cup of coffee and then fucking like minks until dawn, she thanked him for a very nice evening while they were still standing in the lobby of their building.

"I'm so glad we decided to do this," he said.

"Me too," she agreed.

"So, are we still on for dinner on Friday?" he asked.

"Absolutely; I'm looking forward to it."

"Good night, Traci Sanders."

"Good night, Bill Bianco."

Just when Traci thought she would have to wait to find out

what his lips felt like, those strong, yet gentle hands that held onto hers most of the night once again made contact. Before she could take the first step to ascend the three flights of stairs that separated them, he placed his hand over hers on the banister, turned back around and stood squarely in front of her. He caressed both her cheeks and gave her a kiss that, quite literally, took her breath away.

For the first time in a long time she felt like that energized, sexy, enthusiastic girl of her youth.

When their lips separated, Traci decided she hadn't had nearly enough and drew him toward her once again. The connection between them was magnetic and, although she wanted to take things slow and knew that meant it wouldn't be tonight, Traci couldn't wait for the first time their bodies would be joined together.

CHAPTER THREE

hen Traci opened up her computer and saw the instant message from Jennifer, she said out loud, "Note to self, change your instant messenger sign-on name."

"Traci, I am so sorry."

Once again, she was faced with the decision to respond or not to respond. In Jennifer's case she decided to respond.

"Why are you sorry? Because you got caught?"

"No, of course not. I'm sorry that I can't hold my liquor well enough to make better decisions."

There it was, the old, I *did it because I was drunk* excuse. It was Traci's theory that people seldom did anything they wouldn't have done sober. Alcohol didn't *make* you do things. All alcohol did was loosen up a person's inhibitions and offer them up the courage to do something they had already been considering. Traci was convinced that was what had happened between Jennifer and Bryan.

"Whatever."

"I miss you.

"I bet you do. You know, Jennifer, ever since college you have taken from me; my clothes, jewelry, projects for school, food. It never occurred to me that you would start trying to recycle my men as well. I'm all out of stuff to give you. What do you want?"

"Wow, Traci. What has happened to you? I've never seen you

be so unforgiving. Can we at least get together tomorrow to discuss this?"

"Yeah, sure. You're buying."

"No problem."

Traci was very much a daydreamer. This time her daydream was about throwing a drink on some nice dress or suit of Jennifer's while they were having lunch. She wondered if non-lesbian women threw drinks at their girlfriends. Whenever she had seen the dramatic act demonstrated in a film, it was always a woman throwing a drink at a man. Or, she could get shit-faced drunk and throw it at her. Then, she could simply blame it on the alcohol. Hey, under those circumstances, she might even be able to get a bit of food tossed in the mix.

Jennifer was late as usual and Traci considered leaving. After waiting about ten minutes, she arrived.

"I'm sorry I'm late."

Traci said nothing.

"Why do you even bother apologizing? You're always late and you always apologize. Then you just turn right back around and do it all over again. Jennifer, why did you want to get together?"

"I wanted to explain."

"Explain what?"

"What happened with me and Bryan."

"That's water under the bridge. I've met someone else and I feel like maybe you and Bryan happened for a reason. You two deserve each other."

"Wow! You met someone already?"

"Yeah and I'm happy to say that he is nothing at all like Bryan.

"If that's what you want, then I'm happy for you."

"Yes, it is. I'm done with users."

"Traci, are you including me in that comment?"

"Well, you are a user. So, I guess, yes, I am. This was a complete waste of my time. Do me a favor, Jennifer, and lose my instant messenger information and any other form of contact you have to get in touch with me. I'm moving on with my life and making my best efforts to avoid people, like you."

"Fuck you," Jennifer mouthed to Traci as she was walking away.

"Sweety, I wouldn't fuck you with a ten-foot pole. In fact, I'm glad I caught you and Bryan together because you, my dear, are probably riddled with disease."

Traci had never been a woman who enjoyed a scene, but this time she decided to step out of character. She made her comment to Jennifer loud enough for most of the waiters and the people sitting at the surrounding tables to hear.

As she exited the restaurant, fate intervened, and she bumped right into Bill.

"That was quite a show. I can't wait to see the encore presentation."

"I'm afraid that show has been cancelled. It got bad reviews."

Jennifer tried to pretend as if she wasn't watching, but Traci knew she was. The bitch was clearly green with envy and Traci hated to admit it, but she was enjoying every minute of it.

Traci pointed directly at Jennifer without even the slightest bit of fear of reprisal. "You see that woman over there?"

"The one with the red dress, that's trying just a bit too hard?" Bill said, playing along.

"Yeah, that one."

"She pretended to be my best friend and then I came home early one day from work and she was in my bed having sex with my boyfriend."

"Wow, that's really low down. Why were you guys here, together?"

"She wanted to *talk*."

"That's one of those things that should never require a discussion.

Cheaters should never utter the words, *can we talk*. Instead, they should simply slither away and wait it out while they shed their skin."

Traci laughed. Considering how much she was dreading speaking with Jennifer, it turned out to be a perfect day.

Eventually, Jennifer did leave, but not before she shot Bill and Traci a nasty look.

"So, beautiful, do you want to eat here, or somewhere else?"

"Here is fine. Don't you have plans?"

"I had plans to eat lunch alone, but the fates have smiled upon me and instead of eating alone, I'm dining with a beautiful, young woman. Who could ask for anything more than that?"

The conversation between them was stimulating and never seemed to grow cold. There was no searching for the next thing to say or awkward silences. That was what Traci hated about dating. Often, a night out could be as exciting as watching paint dry, but not with Bill. He appeared to be quite multifaceted and open to possibilities.

That first lunch was the first in a long line of many lunches, dinners and lengthy late-night phone calls in the wee hours of the morning.

CHAPTER FOUR

*T*raci and Bill slept peacefully in bed as the morning sun filtered through her bedroom window. She opened her eyes, pressing her body close to his before slowly stroking his awakening manhood. He sighed, contentedly, before speaking.

"Woman, you are going to kill me. We've barely left this room in two days."

"Complaining already? It's only been a couple of months. I can't help it if I want you morning, noon and night. I knew it would be like this from the very first time you kissed me."

"Is that how you remember it? If I remember correctly, you kissed me."

"Bill Giovanni Bianco, you know doggone well you kissed me first."

"That wasn't a kiss. What you gave me; that was a kiss."

"You're nuts."

"That's what you like about me."

"You know what else I like about you? I like the other way you kiss me."

"What other way?"

"Let me show you."

She grabbed a hold of his head and playfully attempted to shove him someplace further south.

"You are absolutely, positively insatiable," he said.

"Your words are saying no, but your body is screaming yes," she pointed out, gently tugging at his quickly growing member.

Her hair fanned out like a lioness as she mounted him. The telltale look of bliss etched across his face encouraged Traci even more. Her lips welcomed him inside of her and held firmly, prolonging the sensation.

"I love you, Traci Sanders," he whispered seductively in her ear.

"I love you, too."

Traci was convinced that what they had was what bliss must feel like. However, lingering somewhere in the back of her mind was the thought that something had to be waiting around the bend to ruin it. True joy seldom went on forever. She wondered what would be the *thing*; that one thing that would be their problem. Every couple had it; something that threatened to break them apart, to ruin the joy. Traci wondered what it would be for her and Bill. The thought plagued her, even as she listened to him singing contentedly in the shower.

"Everything okay?" he asked as soon as he joined her in the bedroom.

"Yeah, everything is fine."

"Liar," he said.

"No, really, I'm fine."

"We haven't known each other that long, but I do know one thing; I know when you're not okay. What's up, baby? You can tell me."

She didn't want to share with him what she was thinking. She was sure she would sound like an irrational fool. "It's nothing. I guess I'm just overwhelmed with work and school and everything," she lied.

Bill knew she wasn't being completely truthful but decided to back off. He hoped that eventually she would share with him what was on her mind.

"So what's for dinner tonight?" she asked.

"Oh, baby, I'm sorry. I forgot to mention; I've got to go to Jersey tonight. My mother needs help with something at the house."

"Oh, okay."

"I'll call you when I'm back in the city. It will probably be late, though. I was going to see what she needed and take her to dinner either before or after, depending on how big the job is."

"No problem."

At least twice a month Bill went to Jersey to help his mother with different odds and ends and never once had he invited her to join him. She didn't want to make a big deal of it and had never brought the subject up to him, but it was starting to bother her. She wondered if she had anything to be concerned about or if she was so accustomed to drama-filled relationships she didn't know how to be in one that was drama-free.

They both left for work that morning, and kissed each other good-bye, as usual. Somehow, though, as they each went their separate ways, Traci felt as though there was something different about that particular kiss.

After a full day of work and school, Traci managed to abandon all thoughts of doom and gloom and when class was over, headed home. She was surprised to see the light on under Bill's door and wondered if his plans had changed. She knocked on the door and was quite surprised when an older woman answered the door. She instantly recognized Bill's mother from the pictures in his apartment.

"Hello, you must be Mrs. Bianco. I've heard so much about you from Bill."

It was obvious to Traci she had no idea who the hell she was.

"Are you one of Bill's neighbors?"

There was no mistaking the look of haughty disdain emblazoned across her face. Traci wondered if it was her in particular that Mrs. Bianco considered inferior, the entire human race in general, or just black folks.

"I live upstairs. Bill mentioned that he was going to visit you in New Jersey."

"He did, did he? Was there something I could help you with, dear?" Mrs. Bianco asked.

Somehow, a term like *dear*, meant to denote affection and endearment, represented nothing but ill-favor when it escaped from her lips. Traci decided it wasn't the human race Mrs. Bianco considered inferior, but her race, in particular. Still, Traci decided she would not stoop to her level and would still interact with her respectfully and kindly.

"No, there's nothing you can help me with. I happened to see the light under the door and I thought I'd stop by and say hello to Bill."

"I'll let him know you stopped by. What did you say your name was?"

"I'm Traci, Traci Sanders."

"Okay, Traci, Traci Sanders. I'll tell him you stopped by.

The door slammed behind her so quickly that if she had lingered any longer, she might have been caught between the hinges.

Once she was downstairs and out of earshot, Traci said the words she had wanted to say ever since first laying her eyes on Bill's mother: "What a bitch!"

By the time the phone rang sometime around 11:00 p.m., Traci was beyond pissed.

"Hi, baby."

"Hello."

"Is everything okay?"

"Everything is fine.

"You don't sound fine."

"Well, I am."

"Are you angry with me about not having dinner with you tonight?"

"I'm not angry; disappointed maybe, but not angry. It is what it is."

"Traci, what gives? You're talking in circles."

"You should know all about that. We spend just about every waking moment together and you profess to love me. Yet, your mother doesn't even know I exist. Did she tell you I stopped by?"

Judging from Bill's reaction, she obviously had not, or maybe he was just a really good liar.

"Uh, no," he stuttered. "She didn't mention that anyone was here."

"Oh, so now I'm anyone. Wow, Darren was right."

"What do you mean, *Darren was right*? I don't even know Darren. What could he possibly have to say about me or us and our relationship?"

"Darren's my brother. He worries about me. He doesn't want to see me being used."

"Is that what you think I'm doing, using you?"

"I didn't think that. Now I'm not so sure. What am I to you? Obviously, I'm not important enough for your mother to know I'm a part of your life, or anyone else for that matter. Or maybe it's that you're ashamed of me. Is that it? Oh my goodness, that's it, isn't it? Are your people racist? Is your mother?"

"Traci, where the hell is all this coming from? I've never met any of your family either."

"My family is spread out all over the world. Of course you haven't met them."

"What about *your* mother? She's a few stops away on the number six train."

"Don't you dare try to turn this thing around on me!"

"Traci, I'm coming up."

"No! I don't want to see you. I'm too upset."

"That's why I want to come up. You shouldn't go to sleep feeling like this."

"Really; you do know that whole don't go to bed angry thing only works if you're actually a couple—and quite obviously that's not us."

Traci hung up the phone and tried to sleep, but it wasn't in the cards for her. She woke up around 2:00 a.m. and tried to do some studying, but couldn't concentrate. Her computer announced an instant message. She already knew who it was. For a moment she considered ignoring it. Instead she tried to see things from Bill's perspective and realized she might have overreacted.

"I'm sorry," the message read.

"Me too," she responded. "Is your mom still there?"

"No, of course she isn't. She left hours ago."

"I'm coming down."

For the first time since they had been together, the sex between them was strained. Traci was preoccupied and concerned that she might have moved way too fast with Bill. The words "implied intimacy" sprang to mind. That was the thing about sex; it made things so very complicated. She couldn't abandon the thought that her value to him was nothing more than incredible sexual compatibility. Traci knew all too well that good sex wasn't enough to maintain a relationship and that once it became obvious there was nothing else, eventually the sex soured as well.

Traci and Bill slept on opposite sides of the bed. They were both engulfed in thought.

By the time Bill woke up in the morning, Traci was gone. He picked up his phone and dialed.

"I've always been there for you, now I need you to do something for me. I'll pick you up at six o'clock tonight. I know you don't want to hear it, but I have to do this. I really do love her."

Sometime around lunchtime there was a delivery for Traci at work, three dozen long-stemmed red roses and a note that read:

"I won't say sorry again because it would be redundant, but I will say you couldn't be more wrong. I love you more than mere words could ever begin to say and will do my very best to prove that to you. I'll pick you up at seven-thirty for dinner."

One of the girls in the office passed by Traci's desk and stopped to admire her flowers.

"Special occasion?" she asked.

"No, nothing like that," Traci responded.

"Either someone's in the dog house or someone is in love. Either way, I say milk it for all it's worth. When you're married as long as someone like me, you almost want to start an argument so you can get a bouquet of flowers every now and then."

Traci's cell phone vibrating was the escape she needed. "I have to take this," she said.

"No problem, girl. Enjoy the flowers."

"Thanks." She picked up the phone. "Hey Darren, long time no talk to. What's been going on?"

"Hey, Baby Girl. You know me; everything is everything."

Traci couldn't help but recognize that Darren sounded like he was talking with a mouth full of marbles.

"Darren, what's wrong with your voice?"

"Nothing's wrong."

"That's bullshit! There's definitely something wrong. You don't even sound the same."

"I'm thinking about coming back to New York."

"Come on, Darren. You're scaring me. What's going on?"

"It's been open season on black folks around here."

"What does that mean?"

"It's nothing serious. A few Mississippi skinheads decided they wanted to beat up some black folks and I happened to enter their radar."

"Are you okay?"

"I got a little bit of a fat lip and my eye is swollen, but otherwise I'm okay. I'll live. It's gonna take a whole lot more than a little-bitty beat-down to scare me."

"That's what I'm worried about, Darren. Does this have anything to do with that group you were telling me about? Color of Change?"

"No. Not really. Our world is changing, baby girl, and not everybody is ready for it."

"Why don't you come home? You're there all alone."

"Well, actually, I'm not really alone."

"Oh my God, did you meet somebody?"

"Yes, I did. You'd like him, Traci. He's really a good guy."

"He better be. Just because I'm a girl doesn't mean I can't whip some ass."

"No, you didn't! Listen to you, ghetto girl."

"Darren, I've got to get back to work. Please promise me you'll stay in touch, okay?"

"No problem. You're gonna get sick of me, I'm gonna be calling you so much."

"Darren, please be careful out there."

"I will. Love you, baby."

"I love you, too."

"Oh, by the way, baby girl, what's his name?"

"What's whose name?"

"The guy you've been seeing."

"How the hell do you do that?"

"I know you very, very well and my memory is long. Don't forget that. The next time we talk I want to hear all about him."

"That is an absolute must."

Traci hurried home and showered and changed into her favorite little black dress. Bill had seen her in it before, but she was sure he would enjoy seeing her in it as much as he had the first time she wore it.

Bill called her and asked that she come down to his place before they left. When she came downstairs, she got the surprise of her life. Sitting in his living room was his mother.

"Hello, Traci," she said.

"Hello, Mrs. Bianco."

Traci took note of the fact that there was no mistaking the absence of the deep freeze she had encountered the first time she met her.

"So Bill, where are we having dinner tonight?" his mother asked.

"It's a surprise. I wanted to take my two favorite girls someplace special."

The drive to New Jersey was pleasant enough and even though Traci was sure Bill probably had to do a lot of convincing to get his mother to join them, she was on her best behavior.

When they arrived at the restaurant, Traci was beyond over-whelmed. The place was incredible. The food was unbelievable and despite the fact that she had eaten more than enough, Traci couldn't resist having dessert.

While they waited for their dessert to arrive, Bill's mother excused herself and went to the ladies room. Traci saw her talking to someone and assumed she had probably run into a friend or maybe even knew the owner of the restaurant. For a moment it almost seemed as though Mrs. Bianco was arguing with the man, but Traci chalked it up to her vivid imagination.

After dessert, it was Traci's turn to excuse herself. Once in the ladies room she realized she had probably overdone it with all the rich food. When she returned to the table, Bill had already paid the check. In the car, Traci began to feel as though something wasn't right. She was violently ill. She didn't know how she was going to make it back from New Jersey to New York in the condition she was in.

"Baby, maybe we should take you to the hospital."

"No, I'm okay. I can make it. It's probably some mild food poisoning."

"Are you sure, dear? Food poisoning can be quite deadly," Bill's mother added.

There was something in her tone that concerned Traci. Just when she thought paranoia and possibly delirium was taking over, her suspicions were confirmed. Upon exiting the car, Mrs. Bianco leaned over and whispered in Traci's ear. "You should be more careful in the future, dear, what you eat and whom you insist on eating it with."

CHAPTER FIVE

*H*er heart sank the moment she saw him. It had been almost a year and she had finally moved on. Yet, here he was standing outside her building, looking as sexy as ever. Before she allowed herself to be sucked in, again, Traci remembered why they were no longer together.

"Bryan, what are you doing here, unannounced?"

"You changed all your numbers. I had no way of getting in touch with you and I had to see you."

"Why? We both said all that needed to be said. How is Jennifer?"

"Traci, don't."

"Don't what? Don't remind you of why I changed my number. Don't ask the obvious question?"

"Traci, it meant nothing. She meant nothing."

"That's the fucked up thing about it," Traci said, slowly raising her voice. "It meant nothing to you to risk everything we had and sleep with my best friend. But, quite frankly, that's all water under the bridge. I lost a lifelong friend and a man I thought cared about me enough not to rip my heart out, but as does usually happen, eventually, I've moved on. So, if you've come here to ease your guilty conscience, you can do that. I forgive you. Now, please leave. Bill will be here soon and I don't want you to be here when he gets home."

"Bill? Who is Bill?"

"The man I've been seeing."

"Oh."

Traci refused to acknowledge the look of hurt in his eyes. She wasn't sure what she was feeling. Was the inner joy she felt at seeing his pain because somewhere deep inside she still had feelings for him, or was it simply that she wanted him to hurt as much as he had hurt her?

"Was there something else?" she asked.

"No, there was nothing else. I was hoping that maybe—"

"Maybe what? That I would be sitting and pining over you when you were done sowing your wild oats? I have one question for you. Why her? Of all the women you could have chosen to fuck, why would you choose to sleep with my best friend and in my own bed?"

"I didn't exactly choose," he whispered.

"Excuse me. Did you actually say you didn't choose? So, what you're trying to tell me is Jennifer pinned you down and made you fuck her."

"Traci, come on."

"Come on and what? You started it. Finish your sentence. You said you didn't choose. What didn't you choose?"

"Clearly, there's no point in this, but I'm going to say what I came here to say. Despite what you may believe, I still care about you, and I always will."

"Spit it out. What exactly did you come here to say?"

"You and I both know Jennifer has issues. She was always jealous of you. I don't think she was ever really your friend. Ever since we were all in college together she dressed like you, took the same classes as you. It's almost like she wanted to be you. When you and I got together, it was no different. This doesn't excuse my behavior, but all the other times I said no."

"All of what other times?"

"Jennifer's been coming on to me since college. It started subtly at first, but through the years her flirtations have grown in intensity. At first I thought she was joking around but after we moved in together she seemed hell bent on getting me into bed."

"You know what I find interesting, Bryan?"

"What, Traci?"

"Through all these years of what you're trying to tell me were ongoing flirtations, you never once said anything to me. Why is that? Why didn't it ever occur to you to say 'hey, baby, your best friend is trying to fuck me?'"

It was difficult for Traci to admit, but memories of how Jennifer would flaunt herself around Bryan were still there. For so long, Traci had chalked it up to low self-esteem or a desire to constantly be in the spotlight, but she never thought she would actually sleep with Bryan.

She remembered one day in particular when they were all at the house together. Jennifer came out of the bedroom wearing nothing but a bra and panties and a short T-shirt. All night she flounced around him, brushing against him. Traci even remembered her telling Jennifer to go put some clothes on. At one point she started teasing Bryan and tried to get him to think about what it would be like if he slept with both of them at the same time. Traci had made it clear that she didn't swing like that, but it still didn't stop Jennifer from toying and teasing all night. Traci realized that because she would never even consider sleeping with a friend's man, it never occurred to her that not everyone possessed such convictions.

"I considered telling you once but then I thought it would hurt you more than help you. I knew how close you and Jennifer were and I thought eventually she would realize I wasn't gonna bite and she would stop."

"But she didn't and you most certainly *did* bite."

"I'm only human. How much can one man take? I come home to find a naked woman in my bed."

"In *our* bed," Traci whispered.

"I'm sorry about that most of all."

"Yeah, sure you are."

"You will probably never believe me, but I am truly, truly sorry. You see, I haven't moved on. I fucked up royally, but I will always love you and I will have to live with that for the rest of my life."

For a moment Traci almost felt sorry for him, that is, until she remembered the pain she had to endure at being betrayed by the man she loved *and* her best friend.

Bryan gazed at her so longingly and with such a show of remorse, Traci was reminded of how things used to be between them. They loved one another once and that love was still hard to forget.

"I'll get to the point of why I came here. Someone mentioned to me that they saw you and Jennifer out together a few weeks ago and I must admit I was surprised. I had to warn you. Traci, that girl means you nothing but harm. Whatever you do, don't trust her."

"I have no intention of trusting her. She wanted to talk and my curiosity got the better of me. I wanted to hear what she had to say. I guess it's the same reason I'm still standing here talking to you," she lied.

In fact, Traci was surprised to find that some of the old feelings she had for Bryan had not gone away and she wasn't too anxious to say good-bye to him yet. Coupled with the fact that things had been a bit rocky between her and Bill since their little dinner with his mother, she was more than a bit confused.

"Bryan, this makes no sense, us standing out here, talking in the street. Come on upstairs."

"What about your boyfriend? Won't he be upset?"

"I'll worry about that."

Once upstairs in her apartment Bryan felt much more comfortable about coming. He wasn't sure what he was walking into, coming to see Traci unannounced, but the fact that she had invited him up proved she still cared for him, even if it probably was just a tiny bit.

"Great apartment; this is what you always wanted. I'm glad you finally got your place in the city. Now all that's left is the beach house."

"I doubt I'll get that on a teacher's salary or an office assistant's salary, for that matter, but I can dream, can't I?"

"Yes, you can. If dreams can't come true for someone like you, the rest of us have no hope."

"What do you mean by someone like me?"

"Despite the way things turned out, Traci, I never stopped loving you or believing in you. You're a good woman and I realize that. I'm an ass, a foolish ass that lost the best thing I ever had."

"Why don't people ever figure that out until it's all over?"

"I don't know, babe. If I knew the answer to that I wouldn't be in the position I'm in now. Speaking of which, who is this guy you're seeing?"

"We met when I was moving in here. He lives in the building."

"Wow, a bit risky, ain't it? When we split up, you didn't want to look at me. Dating someone who lives in the same building as you can be tricky."

"Relationships are tricky, period. I've come to the conclusion that all of that other stuff doesn't matter. It's hard enough finding someone you can connect with and maintain a healthy relationship with, without having a laundry list of unrealistic *deal breakers*. All I do is work and go to school. It makes perfect sense that I would meet someone where I live. If it hadn't been that it would have been someone at school or work. Besides, geography is the least of my problems."

"Really, what is?"

"Well, he's white and I'm pretty sure his family, or at least his mother, isn't particularly fond of black folks, least of all black folks that are dating her son."

"Oh hell no; what does Darren think of this situation?"

"I haven't told him yet. He's had his own issues going on."

"I know, I heard."

"What did you hear?"

"I don't know if Darren told you, but he and I stayed in touch after we broke up. We're both members of this organization that works to assist people of color. It's similar to the NAACP, but it's a bit more progressive. Most of the people who join are much more comfortable with the COC than they are with something like the NAACP. Although the COC deals in politics as well, somehow, it's a lot less *political*, if that makes any sense at all."

"Surprisingly, it does. I get it."

"Well, anyway, Darren and I are both members and the COC chapter in Mississippi is hot; there's all kinds of shit going on in the South that people like you and I wouldn't know a thing about if it weren't for groups like the COC."

"Like what? I'm worried about Darren. You know he got beat up recently."

"Yeah, we heard about that. You know how Darren is. He's your brother. He's always been sort of in your face in his approach to things and that can be real dangerous in places like Greenville, Mississippi."

"I warned Darren about that but he doesn't listen."

"The group has spoken to him as well, but he's hell-bent on

bringing drastic change. I've been trying to speak with him about taking things slow, since I know him better than anyone else. But, Darren's head is hard as a rock."

"Who are you telling? I grew up with that fool."

The two of them laughed.

"This is nice," Bryan pointed out. "I never thought you and I would ever share a laugh about anything ever again."

"Well, if you think that was funny, check this out. I think that old ofay chick, my boyfriend's mother, fucking poisoned me."

"Get the fuck out of here!"

"No shit. I went to dinner with her and her son and not even five minutes after having dessert, I was puking my guts out. Oh, and did I forget to mention that I saw her in a heated exchange with someone at the restaurant. I honestly think she poisoned me or encouraged someone else to do it."

"That shit ain't funny, Traci. What are you doing hanging out with people like that? You're as bad as Darren. That's dangerous."

"I never thought of it as dangerous, per se. It kind of reminded me of something from that old TV show *Dynasty*. You know, Dominique Deveraux and Alexis Carrington, rolling around on the floor and pulling each other's hair."

Traci couldn't help but laugh when she saw the blank look on Bryan's face.

"You know, Diahann Carroll and Joan Collins. They were on a show years ago called *Dynasty*. The show always had these fake-looking girl fights and one time, it was Diahann Carroll and Joan Collins' characters that were doing the fighting."

"Oh, yeah; I remember that show. My mom used to watch it."

Until now, Traci hadn't allowed herself to really believe that Bill's mother had done such a thing, but speaking with Bryan now she was convinced that was exactly what happened.

Bryan and Traci were both unaware of the fact that Bill had come in and heard everything they said about his mother, until he cleared his throat. "Traci?"

"Uh, Bill, this is Bryan. Bryan, this is Bill."

"I've heard a lot about you," Bill said, sarcastically.

"Likewise," Bryan responded.

"Well, I guess I'll be leaving. Traci, think about what I said, okay?"

Bryan made sure he eyeballed Bill as he was leaving.

"I will."

Bryan could hear Bill and Traci arguing as soon as he started downstairs. He wasn't upset at all. He hoped Traci wasn't dealing with some nut job. After all, if a mother was going around poisoning her son's girlfriends, what did that say about the son?

"What the fuck was he doing here?" Bill yelled.

"Excuse me?"

"You heard me. What was he doing here?"

"Some old friends of ours saw me out with Jennifer a few weeks ago and told Bryan. He wanted to warn me to stay away from her. He thinks she might want to do me harm."

"Undoubtedly, she isn't the only person you believe wants to harm you. Did I actually hear you say you thought my mother poisoned you? Are you kidding me? Why would you say a thing like that?"

"I said it because it's true."

"You don't know that."

"Let's put it this way, I'm ninety-nine percent sure she did. Do you know what she whispered to me when she got out of the car that night? She warned me about the consequences of insisting on eating with the two of you."

"I don't believe you."

"Believe whatever you like. Your mother is a racist bitch and she would do anything to keep me away from you."

"You know, Traci, you're painting this picture of my mother as this evil, wicked, crazy person, but you're the one that seems to be surrounded by paranoid delusions."

"Fuck you!"

"You know what, Traci, fuck YOU! I'm done with this. You and people like you are exhausting. You cry racism at every turn, but it wasn't me or my mother using racial slurs, it was you, or don't you think I know what ofay means?"

"The difference between people like me and people like you and your mother is that I only lash out when being attacked. I didn't have to do anything more than show up at your door for her to treat me like garbage. Your mother might as well be a card-carrying member of the Klan, but if you asked her I'm sure she would profess to be the farthest thing from a racist. And you, you sit around with your buddies in the office making jokes about niggers, spicks and wetbacks in one breath and in the next claim to be liberals. Tell me one thing, when you're sitting around engaging in *nigger* jokes, do you ever mention me?"

As far as Traci was concerned, the blank look on his face was all she needed to know. She had nothing more to say. With that said, Bill walked out, slamming the door as hard as he could behind him.

CHAPTER SIX

*O*nce again she was alone, only this time she had to see the man she had broken up with every day. That was the downside to dating someone who lived in the same building. She did everything she could to avoid running into him and for a while it worked, until she ran into him early one morning with a woman in tow.

"Hello, Traci."

"Hello, Bill. How are you?"

"Oh, I'm...I'm good. How's the job?"

"It's great, the best job I've had in a long time. I'm almost finished with school. Hopefully, I'll be teaching soon."

"Oh, Traci, that's great. I know how much you've wanted to teach."

For a moment both Traci and Bill seemed to forget they weren't alone until the leggy blonde with Bill suddenly grabbed his arm and spoke. "Bill, we should probably get going if we want to have breakfast before we go to work."

Traci thought she looked familiar. It was the same coworker she had joked with Bill about. Somehow she knew she wanted him. For the life of her she couldn't understand why some women seemed to find men so much more attractive when they were with someone else. After all, she had worked with him for years. Why did she decide to pounce as soon as he was involved with someone else?

As if Bill's coworker suddenly read her thoughts, she acknowledged

Traci for the first time. "I don't know if you remember me. I'm Eleanor. We met at the firm Christmas party."

"Yeah, I remember you," Traci answered dryly.

Traci wanted to scratch her fucking eyes out. Her reminding Traci that they had met before was merely a way of marking her territory. It was like pointing out to Traci that she had won. The words karma is a bitch was all Traci needed to remember to soothe her bruised heart.

"It was nice seeing you, Traci," Bill said. "I hope you get the teaching assignment you want."

"Yeah, me too; don't worry, I'll keep you posted. After all, we are neighbors."

Traci couldn't resist reminding Eleanor that she had the home court advantage.

"Bill, didn't you mention to Traci that you're moving?"

"No, I guess I didn't. I found an incredible loft on the West Side, right near The Empire State Building. This place was always only temporary until I could find someplace to settle in."

"Yeah, I remember."

What Traci remembered was all their talks about the future. Once upon a time, she thought she and Bill might enjoy a future together. She wondered if Eleanor was moving in with him, but decided the three of them standing uncomfortably in the lobby was more than she could stand.

"Good luck, Bill."

"Good luck to you, Traci."

"Yes, good luck," Eleanor added.

Traci was halfway out the door when Eleanor spoke. She was anxious to escape before she gave Eleanor a piece of her mind or a piece of her fist. The thought of her and Eleanor rolling around in the lobby of the building all dressed up and ready for work, while

Bill tried to intervene, surprisingly, brought a smile to her lips.

After running into Eleanor and Bill, avoiding him became a full-time job for Traci. She was working a great deal and actively pursuing a teaching job. By the time she laid her head on her pillow at night she was exhausted. Unfortunately, she couldn't avoid moving day for Bill. Things had ended so abruptly for the two of them and she knew it wasn't truly over for either of them. She was convinced of that fact the morning of his move when he knocked at her door. It was Saturday morning, the only day of the week she slept in. When she opened the door, she was still wearing plaid pj's and her fuzzy bunny slippers.

Bill chuckled as soon as he saw her. "I think what I'm going to miss most of all are those slippers."

In her haste to answer the door she had forgotten she was even wearing them. In spite of the pain she felt in anticipating what she knew was going to be a good-bye, she couldn't help but look down at her feet and laugh herself.

"You know I..."

Traci put a finger to his lips and the sleepy, sexy look he got in his eyes, that same look she enjoyed so immensely when they made love, almost stopped her. Somehow, she continued, knowing that if it were meant to be it would. She hoped their paths would cross again, but if they did not, then it probably wasn't meant to be.

"I understand," she continued. "You don't have to say the words. I feel the same way."

His smile was forced and seemed full of regret, but she allowed him to leave without saying anything further. After closing the door, she spent the rest of the day in her bed crying. On Sunday she decided she had felt sorry for herself long enough and would get out of the house and go have brunch. Before she left the building she couldn't help but stop downstairs and try the door to

Bill's now vacant apartment. She was happy to find the door was open and even happier to find that Bill had been thinking of her as well. There was a note left on the island in the kitchen, addressed to her.

Dear Traci,

It's funny the things you can say in a letter that you can't say to a person face-to-face. I feel as though I've spent my entire life looking for someone exactly like you, but the moment I found you, somehow I knew it wasn't our time. I believe we'll find our way back to one another once again, when we're both ready. Always know that I do love you and our not being together is nothing more than bad timing, unfinished business and a world that's not ready for a love as spectacular as ours. I'll be here whenever you need me, whenever you want me. Much Love. Bill

Just when Traci thought she had no more tears left, there were the water works once again. She decided she was not in the best frame of mind for brunch alone and returned to her apartment and the comfort of her bed.

It took some time but, after a few months, she returned to feeling close to normal. She had gotten a teaching job in Harlem and was happy to be working someplace where she might actually make a difference. Unlike many of her black colleagues who felt somehow slighted when they were sent to work at some of the lowest scoring schools in some of the worst neighborhoods in New York, Traci was buoyed by the prospect of teaching in an environment where she could have the greatest impact. It didn't take long for her to figure out that the educational system, like so many other facets of life, was uneven for those most in need. Unlike so many of the schools in more affluent neighborhoods where she had worked as a student teacher, the schools uptown were sorely lacking when it came to funding, curriculum and teacher motivation. It was as if the children there were being set up for a fall. Traci was convinced she could change all of that. As was usually the case for teachers, one child in particular stood out in her mind. His name was Kevin and she was hell bent on *saving* him.

For the life of her Traci couldn't understand why Kevin Smith was walking around in what she knew were two-hundred-dollar athletic shoes but his mother insisted their family couldn't afford to buy the supplies he needed for school. She did everything she could to help, including providing him with many of the supplies he needed.

"You do know you can't save them all," the school's principal cautioned her one day.

"But I can try, can't I?"

"The root of the problem goes farther back than anything we can fix."

"And here I thought nothing was incapable of being fixed."

"I almost forgot what it was like to be an idealistic new teacher. You'll learn. After working here long enough you'll figure out how deep-seated the problem really is."

"I'm listening."

"I heard you comment in the teacher's lounge about how many of the kids here are wearing expensive shoes and designer clothing, but show up unprepared with the most basic school supplies. Do you know why that is? It's a mindset that started long before any of us were born. So many in this community, and others like it, still operate from that very same mindset.

"Which is?"

Sandra Piper, the school's principal, sensed Traci's agitation, but felt she needed to hear the truth. "Do you know what I did before I became a teacher?"

"No, I don't."

"I worked for the Welfare Office or you probably know it as

The Department of Social Services or the Human Resources Department. Any way you slice it, I still see it as institutionalized slavery. I see the look on your face, so let me first say that I have no judgment around those needing help. Unfortunately, the whole system is awry. Human beings need to be able to care for themselves and that can't happen if the dysfunctional cycle continues. I can remember women coming in to apply for services with their nails done, their hair weaved and coifed and wearing designer clothes, but there they were applying for welfare. There has to be something wrong with that picture. Many of these women continued to come back time and time again having baby after baby that they couldn't afford. They couldn't afford to feed their children, but they could afford two hundred dollars to weave their hair and designer duds. It goes way back to the time of slavery. You know the old story. There were those who worked the fields and those who got the *easier* work inside the big house. Those inside ate better and dressed better. Some even endeared themselves so to the *master* that they eventually were afforded some of the finer things, at least by slavery standards. Some, in fact, were able to induce their *owners* to grant them their freedom. Is it any wonder that the ownership of *things* became a symbol of prosperity? What still fascinates me is that many of us have no conscious awareness of how and why this way of thinking could live on. Of course it lives on. The desire for the best designer labels, even in the face of poverty, seems ridiculous, but it makes perfect sense to me. Until the way of thinking is changed, the behavior will continue, and in fact it has continued, for generations, and it will go on and on for generations to come until the cycle is broken."

"You remind me of my brother, Darren. His belief system is very similar to yours."

"I would love to meet this brother of yours. He sounds like a man worth knowing."

"I must admit, he is. He's my brother, and I don't always agree with what he has to say, but I commend him for his convictions. He's extremely passionate about his beliefs. That's one of the things I love most about him."

"You are quite lucky, Ms. Sanders, and now I feel lucky as well."

"Why?" Tracy asked.

"It's only a matter of time before you begin to see things for what they are. Between your brother and me, I guarantee your perspective will begin to change sooner rather than later. Then this army will have another soldier."

"Army?"

"That's exactly what it is. It's a war. It's no different than any other war. Our people, people of color, are merely fighting for survival. What frightens me most in this fight is that most of us don't have a clear picture of the casualties. We've become so numb to what we consider commonplace occurrences; the abject poverty, death and destruction, that there are many that don't even know there's a war going on."

Traci was speechless.

"I don't know what to say, Ms. Piper. I guess in many respects I'm one of those people you're talking about who is unaware. I've often thought of my brother as a bit of a fanatic when he speaks to me in exactly the same way you have today."

"Do you consider me a fanatic as well?"

"I'm not sure why, but I don't. What you just told me didn't ring of fanaticism. However, it did scare me."

"Then what I told you worked. That was my goal. You need to be scared. With fear comes awareness. An unaware teacher, even an idealistic one, is useless."

As if on cue, the bell announcing next period rang.

"Nice having you on board," said Principal Piper.

"Thank you."

Traci really was afraid. If she were to believe what the principal had shared with her, what was the point...of any of this? What could any one of them, her, Darren, the principal, truly do to halt wheels that had already been set into motion long ago?

Then she remembered the President of the United States' original campaign slogan: *Yes We Can!* She wondered if it was truly possible to enact such great change in the face of such adversity. As she mulled this over in her head, she watched as a drug deal went down between two students and knew at that moment that no effort was too great. There was a whole community of people who were slowly dying and she couldn't stand idly by and watch it happen. She was energized and couldn't wait for the opportunity to call Darren and share with him what her day at school had been like. She was so excited she couldn't wait. She picked up the phone and dialed his number. He was at work and she would most likely get his voicemail, but she couldn't wait.

While simultaneously waiting for Darren's voicemail to kick in and for the second school bell to ring, declaring she was late for class, she instead got a message on the phone announcing that all circuits were busy and a warning alarm within the school signaling that there was an emergency. Before she had an opportunity to speculate, Principal Piper exited her office and began walking vigorously toward her. Despite her obvious air of professionalism, there was no mistaking the sense of alarm written upon her face. She walked up to Traci and leaned in close, whispering in her ear.

"There's been an explosion and it's really bad. The Empire State Building was bombed."

Traci's first thought was of Bill. She searched her wallet for the letter he left her when he moved out of the building. She remembered that his address was included in the letter...Five East Thirty-Fourth Street. His home was right near the Empire State Building. It was as if all the oxygen had been sucked out of the room. She couldn't breathe.

"Traci! Are you okay? Traci, can you hear me?"

From a distance she could just barely hear the principal speaking.

"I'm sorry, Principal Piper, but I've got to go."

"Ms. Sanders, you can't go. I'm going to need you. We've got children here to attend to."

"But..."

Principal Piper fully understood. It was 9/11 all over again. Obviously, Traci had a loved one that either worked in or was near the Empire State Building, but there was really nothing she could do at this juncture. For now, they would all have to stay put.

"Traci, I understand, but for now we've all got to keep our heads and not go off half-cocked. Do you have a loved one in the building?"

"Yes, I mean, no. Not in it but right next to it. He recently moved there."

"I'm going to turn on the news in the staff lounge and we all need to go over for the protocol put in place for dispatching all of the kids safely."

"Okay. I'm sorry."

"Don't apologize. I understand. These are and will be trying times. Your reaction was perfectly normal."

Many parents showed up to take their kids home and for those who didn't there was protocol put in place for what would happen with the kids if it were unclear about the status of their parents. There was a possibility that some of the kids might have had parents that worked in or near the Empire State Building or even lived near there, although most of the kids at MS 344 lived in the same West Harlem neighborhood.

"The Department of Education is reaching out to parents and we can enact our automated phone system to notify parents of what is happening. In the meantime, most of the children have been released. I am going to stick around and I will need some of you to stay, but if there are teachers who need to leave you can do that in the next half-hour or so," Principal Piper announced. "Traci, you can leave now."

"Thank you. Thank you so much!"

Traci was shocked when her phone rang. It was Darren.

"Baby girl, are you okay?"

"I'm fine, but I'm worried about Bill. The city is a mess. There are people crying and the news is horrendous. The building is obliterated."

"We're watching the news here now. Traci, please tell me you're not planning on doing anything crazy like going down there?"

"I have to find him."

"Traci, please be realistic. Even if you could get anywhere near there, it's not a good idea."

Darren was right, but she felt so helpless. Entry in and around the city was impossible. It dawned on her that her own apartment was only seven blocks away. She wasn't even sure she'd be able to get home. Everything was stopped. Buses and trains weren't running and cabs were impossible. Her adrenaline in overdrive, she walked in the direction of home, practically on autopilot. When she finally came to her senses, she looked up and realized she was only blocks away. She stuck her key in the lock to the building's entrance and Bill fell into her arms. He was covered in soot and looked like he was in shock but as far as she could tell he was otherwise okay. She grabbed him, hugging him close to her, kissing his cheeks his forehead, his eyelids, his lips. He was alive!

"Oh my God, Bill, I thought I had lost you!"

CHAPTER SEVEN

School was closed the next day and for the rest of the week the number of students and teachers in attendance was sparse. Traci had hoped many of the children had been spared the impact of the devastation that was to follow, since the school was so far away from where the explosion had occurred.

Unfortunately, there were some families within their small community that had been affected. There were parents, family members and friends who had still not been located and were believed to be dead. It was heart-wrenching. Any pain she thought she felt, at first losing Bryan and then Bill, was nothing compared to what some of these families were going through. She watched the news and cried for the pain the destruction had caused so many. After two days of watching nothing else but the coverage of what was believed to be a terrorist attack, she realized she couldn't watch anymore.

Bill still appeared to be experiencing some level of shock and, despite Traci's efforts to encourage him to talk about it, for the first couple of days he was mostly resistant. However, after spending most of his time sleeping and the rest moving about like a zombie, he began to slowly rehash the events of that fateful day.

"I've never seen anything like it. One minute I was walking down Fifth Avenue. There were people everywhere, as usual. Tourists with cameras around their necks lined the street and I was trying to push my way past them to get where I was going, then it was like the earth opened up. I can still hear the sound of it reverberating in my ears, and suddenly there was a hole where that great big landmark used to be. How? How could anything so apparently strong be destroyed so quickly and so easily? I can't wrap my head around what's happened. I feel like even now I still can't think clearly. The only thing that was clear to me then and still is now is that my first thought was of you. In the midst of it all I couldn't help but think of that beads store right on Fifth Avenue that you love to shop at...loved to shop at. I don't even think it's there anymore. I remember thinking 'please don't let her be in that store. Please God don't let her be in there.' I started walking and I ended up here. I rang all the bells and someone opened up the door. I don't even know who it was. I was so incredibly tired. I can't remember ever feeling so tired. I leaned against the door and the first person to open it from the other side was you. It was you!"

In the weeks and months to follow there were all sorts of theories about who had caused the devastation. Unlike the 9/11 terrorist attacks, no one had taken credit. However, eventually, links to al-Qaeda were apparently confirmed. Who caused the explosion had not been the only mystery. It was theorized that numerous packages containing high explosives and detonators controlled by a radio receiver had caused the catastrophe. However, the question still remained as to how so many packages of explosives could have been hidden in a building possessing such a high level of security? The other question was, where were the individuals stationed who controlled the remote controls necessary to cause the detonations? Talk of an inside job ran rampant.

As the country began the process of healing, new threats of war became a reality. After nearly fifteen years, U.S. troops had finally been pulled out of Afghanistan. Now it appeared it would be little more than a yo-yo effect.

"Do we have to keep watching this? I could think of a lot of better things we could be doing," Bill said, seductively.

"Whoo, hoo! Look who's getting frisky. I don't know, Mr. Bill. That news guy sure is sexy. You sure you can compete with that bouffant and blue suit?"

"Hell yeah; I've got gifts Mr. Newsman will never be able to compete with!"

Bill shut off the television and turned on the radio and executed an impressively seductive striptease.

"Do the thing, do the thing!" Traci cheered.

"Yeah, baby! I know what you want!"

Bill disappeared for a few minutes and when he came back, he was soaking wet.

"Do it! Do it! Do it!" Traci continued to chant.

Bill jumped up on the coffee table and continued gyrating.

"Don't bust your ass now," Traci joked.

"You might be right."

He jumped off the table and continued to move seductively to the music.

"Are you gonna do the move or what?"

"Okay, baby, here it is. You sure you're ready for this?"

"I'm ready."

Bill proceeded to attempt to rip his wet T-shirt from his body. When it didn't work as easily as it appeared to in wet T-shirt contests they had both seen on TV, he disappeared again.

"I'll be right back."

He came back with a scissor and cut the T-shirt straight down the middle, before ripping the rest in half.

"You are my hero, Mr. Bianco!"

They convulsed in a fit of laughter.

"I missed this?"

"What?" Traci asked.

"This; I missed us and just having fun with you. I've never had this much fun with anyone before you or since you."

"Not even Eleanor?"

"Definitely not Eleanor; her idea of a good time was finding out what our coworkers just bought and going out and buying something bigger, better and more expensive. Eleanor was a bit transparent."

"I'm glad to hear you say it."

"Can I tell you something without you getting angry?"

"Go for it."

"When she was here that time, right before I moved and you guys were sparring, or should I say, doing the female version of a pissing contest, my first thought was I hope I don't have to break up a fight between these two, then I started thinking, I wonder who would win?"

"I would have kicked her tight ass."

"Listen to you."

"Listen to you. What is it with men and chick fights anyway? Besides, she had it coming. She was checking you out when we went to your company Christmas party. I get it now, though. She's one of those ultra-competitive types. I bet you she was a gymnast."

Bill laughed.

"She was, wasn't she?"

"Yes! You ever consider becoming a psychologist?"

"Funny you should ask. The thought has crossed my mind. For now I think I'll utilize my *gift* in the New York City public school system. Believe you me, it's greatly needed. Speaking of which, I know you're feeling better, but have you considered speaking with someone about your recent experience?"

"You're all the counseling I need, Kitten."

"That's flattering, but there are those out there who are even more skilled than me."

Bill suddenly got a serious look on his face. "Traci, don't worry about me. I'm fine."

"Okay, no pressure."

"I do need to find an apartment, though."

"Why can't you just stay here?" she asked.

"Really? Why, Traci Sanders, are you asking me to move in with you?" Bill said coyly.

"Yeah, move in with me."

"I didn't think you'd ever ask. Wanna christen the bed? Huh, huh, wanna!"

"I swear, you are like a little kid sometimes. Yes, we can bone now. Although, I do believe we've christened this bed many, many times before."

"That was when we were dating, now we're living together. That's a different story altogether."

"Wow, some people will say anything for a great roll in the hay."

"Hey, you didn't tell me you had hay, too. I'm gonna love it here," he joked.

"Baby, I've got secrets you haven't even seen yet. Come here. Let me show you a couple of them."

Traci pulled Bill to her and devoured those lips she had come to adore.

"Wow, Kitten, when you kiss me like that, I can barely think."

"You don't need to think. Everything we're going to do tonight will come as naturally as breathing."

"You keep kissing me like that and I won't be able to breathe either."

"Then maybe I should give your lips a rest and concentrate on kissing some other neglected areas."

The intensity of her lips on his body was almost more than Bill could stand. He kept rising up from the bed, trying to return the joy he was giving her.

"Relax," Traci whispered. "I have so much I want to show you, not the least of which is how very much I've missed you. Just lay back, baby. I missed your body so much I have an overwhelming urge to worship it tonight."

"No complaints here," he added.

Traci made good on her promise. She spent the entire night showering him with adoration, from the top of his head to the tip of his toes. She didn't realize how much she had missed him until he was inside of her. When she eventually reached full tilt, the intensity of her orgasm was enough to illicit tears of joy.

The next morning Traci was happy to see that Bill was still sleeping peacefully. Ever since the explosion he had been experiencing terrible nightmares and often he was up pacing the floors, unable to sleep. She decided she would make him a nice breakfast. Unfortunately, the cupboards were bare. She decided to make a quick run to the supermarket and get some things for the week.

When she returned, she was surprised to find Bill's mother sitting on the edge of *her* bed, next to Bill, who was now wide awake.

"Hello, dear."

"Hello," Traci responded flatly.

"Thank you so much for allowing my son to come and stay with you while he sorts this terrible business out. We had some business to discuss, so I thought I'd use the opportunity to stop by and thank you personally."

Traci was so happy to be reunited with Bill, she had somehow forgotten about his shrew of a mother. She hoped these little visits wouldn't get to be a habit and held on to the hope that the divide separating New Jersey from New York was wide enough to keep her away.

"Oh, it's no problem at all. I'm glad he's here."

"Bill, get up and help the girl with her bags!"

Traci kept thinking how everything that rolled off this woman's tongue somehow seemed laced in venom. She could make even a simple word like *girl* sound offensive.

"I just wanted you to know that I appreciate it."

Traci wondered what Bill had told his mother. Something about the way Mrs. Bianco spoke sounded more like she was helping out a former neighbor in need, and not a boyfriend and girlfriend simply living together. Traci decided that Bill had been through enough and that it wasn't worth bringing up.

"Mrs. Bianco, will you stay and have breakfast with us?"

"Oh no, dear; that's so kind of you, but I only planned to stop by for a quick talk with Bill. I have another appointment."

Traci hoped her smile didn't betray her true thoughts. It occurred to her that if she were Mrs. Bianco, she wouldn't eat anything she cooked either. That was the thing about poisoning someone; you had to constantly lay in wait for the person to return your evil deed.

"Maybe another time," Traci added.

"Why of course," Mrs. Bianco agreed. "Bill, honey, I hope you don't become a burden on Ms. Saunders."

"Mom, her name is Sanders, Traci Sanders."

"I'm so sorry, dear. I'm terrible with remembering names. Now, a face, that's a different story. I never forget a face."

CHAPTER EIGHT

*I*t took some time, but eventually the city itself and life for Bill and Traci returned to normal. Traci was happy that Bill's mother did not make it a habit of stopping by. She was always relieved when Bill drove out to New Jersey to visit her; that meant Mrs. Bianco would not be sitting in her living room. However, as she expected, all good things eventually come to an end.

"My mom would like us to come to dinner next Sunday," Bill said.

Somehow, the two of them had managed to ignore the giant purple elephant in the room. When they split up, it had been because Traci believed Bill's mother had poisoned her and Bill refused to admit his mother might be capable of something so horrible. Neither of them had changed their opinion. Yet, under the present circumstances, they both knew either they were going to talk about it or ignore it.

"Dinner is fine."

"I'll call her and let her know."

Although a smile was pasted on Traci's face, she was actually thinking, "Sure, that will give her more of an opportunity to figure out how best to poison me by Sunday."

Traci couldn't wait to tell Darren about her plans for the weekend. Given how things had turned out the last time Bill overheard her talking about his mother, she decided to call Darren from someplace other than home.

"What, no school today?" Darren asked as soon as he answered the phone.

"It's my lunch break. I didn't want to call from home."

"Why not; who are you shacking up with? Is it Bryan or Bill?"

"You suck."

"That's what they say," Darren joked.

"Ew, you are so nasty and that is way too much information. I wanted to tell you and then you go and ruin it."

"You still haven't told me. Who is it?"

"Bill, of course."

"You say that like it's completely impossible that it could be Bryan. You know you still love that man."

"You and I both know that love isn't always enough. He's a cheater and he's selfish. Not only did he cheat on me but he cheated with my best friend. I don't think I will ever be able to forgive that."

"I hear you. I've been cheated on. Believe me, I know how much it hurts, but as far as that heifer, Jennifer, she is no friend. She never was. I couldn't stand her ass from the first day I met her. I tried to warn you about her, but no, you didn't want to listen to me. When are you going to believe what I say when I tell you I can see through people very easily? Jennifer's shit was more transparent than most. I used to watch her around Bryan and your other friends' men. She's one of those insecure sisters who can't feel good about herself unless she's fucking around with somebody else's man. This time it just happened to be yours. Women like that can never truly be anybody's friend. They're too interested in what it is they need and want to care about anyone else's feelings."

"Did I tell you she tried to smooth things over with me?"

"You didn't tell me, but Bryan did."

"By the way, when did you and Bryan get so chummy?" Traci asked.

"I've always liked Bryan. He's a good guy. Clearly, he doesn't always make the best decisions, but who does? Speaking of which, what's up with you and this Bill character? What's that about?"

"Why did you say it like that?"

"I'm just being honest. I've only heard bits and pieces about him from you; Bryan mentioned that he met him when he visited you."

"See, now I know how you know so much about me. It's not instinct at all. It's because you've got your spies out watching me."

"Yeah, it's that too. But, it's also because I do know you very well. So, stop changing the subject. What's up with the white boy?"

"Darren, come on. Can you at least try to be more P.C.?"

"Didn't I tell you? I lost my ability to be politically correct when I moved to Greenville, Mississippi."

"What is it that you want to know? I can't imagine that there's anything left that Bryan or any of your other spies haven't told you already," Traci said.

"There are some things that even the best spies don't know, like do you really love this guy?"

"I do, Darren. I really do."

"So you're telling me you love him enough to risk life and limb. That must be some good stuff."

"I see you've been talking to Bryan."

"I think she's just an overprotective mother."

"Is that what you really believe?"

"That's why I was calling you. I wanted your opinion, but you beat me to the punch."

"What do you want my opinion on?"

"I'm assuming Bryan mentioned to you that I think she did something to my food at a restaurant we went to."

"Actually, the word Bryan used was *poisoned*," said Darren.

"That's not Bryan's fault. That was my word. That's what it felt like when it happened. Now, I'm thinking maybe it was just a mother scared of losing her only son."

"Baby girl, you know I never tell you what to do."

"Since when do you, of all people, never tell me what to do!"

"Well, this time I won't tell you what to do. I will say this, though; watch your back. In my experience, crazy doesn't usually take a holiday, at least not for long."

By the time Sunday arrived, Traci was a bit nervous. She wasn't sure if she was more concerned about her physical well being or interacting with Mrs. Bianco.

"What do you think of this one?" Traci asked.

"It's just as beautiful as the other ten outfits you tried on. You could wear a potato sack and you'd still look gorgeous."

"I bet that would go over big. That's what I'll do. I'll show up at your mother's house in a potato sack."

Traci finally settled on a simple black sheath dress when it was apparent that they would be very late if she didn't choose something immediately. She spared no detail, down to the makeup, which she seldom wore. By the time she finished applying her makeup, Bill was waiting patiently.

"You sure you wanna go to this thing?" Bill asked.

"Are you kidding me? After all this, of course I want to go."

Bill eased up behind Traci and stroked her legs.

"Bill, stop it! You're going to rip my pantyhose. Then I'll have to start all over again, and we will be late."

"I can't help it. Your curves in that dress are driving me crazy."

"Cut it out, you nut. We've got to go."

The ride to New Jersey was surprisingly quiet. Traci was understandably nervous and Bill was hoping there would be no need for him to mediate.

"So how long has your mother lived here?" Traci asked.

"She's been here my entire life."

"Oh wow, so you grew up here. I can't wait to see the home you ran around in when you were in diapers."

"I'd rather see yours."

"Do you really want to see where I grew up?"

"Why wouldn't I?"

"Well, if you want to see where I grew up, we'll have to make that happen."

The further they drove, the more Traci kept thinking they were lost; the opulence of the homes was unmistakable. She didn't expect poverty, but she was completely unprepared for this. One house stood out from all the rest. It was the closest thing to a mansion Traci had ever seen up close. She held her breath as Bill pulled up in front of it.

"Here?"

Before Bill had an opportunity to respond, Eleanor came running over to the car.

"Bill, how are you? Are you okay?"

"I'm fine, Eleanor. How are you?"

"I'm better now that you're here. Traci," she said, in lieu of a hello.

"Eleanor," Traci responded.

Traci couldn't believe she was there and wondered what else Mrs. Bianco had in store for her. From the moment she walked through the front door she realized saying she was in the minority would have been the definition of an understatement.

Mrs. Bianco breezed toward her and Bill, her shift billowing behind her.

"Oh Bill, I'm so glad you could make it. This wouldn't be a party without you here. Oh, hello dear," she said to Traci.

"Hello, Mrs. Bianco."

The attendees at the party were a Liberal's nightmare. Most of her guests were self-centered, over-indulged assholes. As if that wasn't enough, Bill was nowhere to be found. Traci wondered how long she would have to stay before she feigned a terrible headache and went home. Just when she thought her ears were oozing brain matter, a kind voice spoke.

"Maybe I should get you another drink before you start sucking on the ice."

It was the first time Traci had laughed since she walked through the door.

"I was right, wasn't I? The ice was next. Wait here. I'll be right back."

Within a couple of minutes, the tall, attractive gentleman with the 100-watt smile returned, carrying two glasses.

"This is for you, Milady."

"Thank you."

"You look like you are having an absolutely *wonderful* time," he mentioned, sarcastically.

"How can you tell?"

"Body language says it all; the shifting of feet, the fingering of the empty glass, the blank stare. None of these things are a good sign. Is there anything I can do? You look lost."

"Do you know the hostess?" Traci asked.

"Candace? Yes, I know her. Don't you? Or are you a gate crasher?"

"I am *definitely* not a gate crasher. I'm her son's girlfriend."

"Are you really?"

"Yes. Do you know Bill?"

"I know him quite well."

"I'm Traci Sanders."

"Hello, Traci. I'm Anthony."

"Hello, Anthony. So, do you come to a lot of Mrs. Bianco's parties, and are they always like this?"

"Yes, they are, always like this. If you're going to be spending time with Bill, you should probably get used to it."

"Either this or coming up with very good excuses to leave. I find headaches work quite well in just about any situation."

"Not this one. You'll learn." Anthony glanced at his clock. "We'll be sitting down to dinner in a few minutes. You seem like a nice person so I hope you don't mind if I give you a bit of advice."

"What's that?"

"Whatever you do, don't show Mrs. Bianco any fear *or* even try confronting her, for that matter. Both would be serious mistakes. She tramples the weak and her sense of superiority won't allow her to permit anyone to disagree with her in any way. She may not look it, but she can be quite a challenging adversary and despite Bill's strong demeanor, he's putty in his mother's hands. Mind you, that's just my perspective. You can do with it what you will."

"Thanks, Anthony, I'll do that."

"Oh, let me cue you in on one more thing."

"What's that?"

"Be careful about what you say around these people. They're all sheep and they follow her blindly."

"I'll keep that in mind."

Before they could sit down to dinner, Traci noticed the housing staff whispering to one another. All of their faces seemed alarmed and one appeared to have been crying. It wasn't long before everyone would learn what had happened. Two guests arrived and announced the news.

"The President has just been shot!" one of them said.

CHAPTER NINE

For the first twenty minutes or so Bill and Traci drove back from New Jersey in silence. The only sound to be heard was that of Traci's intermittent sniffles. She couldn't believe he was dead. After several minutes of crying, Traci was struck by the fact that Bill hadn't reacted at all; not even to ask if she was okay. It was odd. It was as if he were trying his very best to avoid the subject.

"Doesn't this upset you at all?" Traci suddenly asked.

"It does, but I don't think it upsets me in the same way it does you."

"What does that mean?" Traci asked, through her tears.

"Our political beliefs are really different. Even though we don't discuss it much, I've always known that. What concerns me more than the President being murdered is how this whole scenario is going to play itself out. It's my prediction that it will forever divide this country."

"This country is already divided. It's always been divided. It became divided the moment human beings became property. I could discover the cure for AIDS, yet I would still be the black woman that discovered the cure for AIDS. Martin Luther King, Jr. was an incredible man; a man for all people. However, his holiday is still thought of as a black holiday. I'll never be considered equal, at least not in this lifetime. Sadly, I've had to get used to that. I love you and I know that you love me, but when all is said and done, can you with all honesty say that as a white man, you consider me, a black woman, an equal?"

"Do you really have to question that?"

"Absolutely; each time the President ran for election it was more about race than it was about *the* race. Can it be possible that a couple whose meeting was simultaneous with the President of The United States being elected, have never discussed politics?" Traci asked.

"That's completely possible. Does that bother you?" said Bill.

"It does bother me a little."

"Why? Even couples don't agree on everything."

"But Bill, don't you think politics is a pretty important thing to agree on? It's a major component of all of our lives. Yet, even in that race was a factor. The fact that the presidential candidate was black made it difficult for both of us to discuss our choice for election."

"I've never been terribly political. I've always gotten the impression that you aren't either. Most couples end up discussing those things they're most passionate about most often. Maybe this isn't something either of us is truly passionate about. Correct me if I'm wrong."

"You're not wrong, Bill. I'm not hugely political but somehow when a black man was nominated for the presidential election, I began to think more about my political convictions, or should I say lack thereof. He represented something for my people and me. For most black people he represented hope. When I voted for him, that's what I felt. I felt hope for what the future could hold for not only me, but for every black person that believed there were still unspoken limits to our equality."

"I don't think I've ever heard you talk like this. *Your people*; what does that even mean?"

"We don't discuss race often, but there is a reality to the impact of color differences. It has a lot to do with the lives we lead and the decisions we make, both political and otherwise."

"I've never thought of it that way," Bill admitted.

"Are you serious? Are you telling me you really don't think color makes a difference? I can remember having this conversation with a coworker many years ago. She was adamant about her comparison of the trials and tribulations of Blacks and Jews. It was her contention that it wasn't an issue of race but an issue of differences. She also pointed out to me that the suffering and discrimination of Jews, both past and present, was at least equal to Blacks and, in her opinion, Jews had suffered more and were discriminated against more than Blacks. I pointed out to her that even in a cosmopolitan, and apparently forward-thinking city such as New York, I still had more difficulty getting a taxi to pick me up than my white counterparts. I explained to her that although taxi drivers probably seldom looked at her and thought *I'm not picking up that Jew*, they often looked at me and others like me and thought *I'm not picking up that black person*."

"In all the years we've been together I don't think I've ever heard you play the race card."

"The race card; what does that mean? It's not a card. It's a fact. And, the thing about being Black is you get so used to it you forget to be truly angry unless you're especially hard-hit."

Before going to bed, Traci turned on *ABC News*.

"This is a recording of this afternoon's shooting of both the President and Vice President at the Washington Hilton Hotel. Here you see the President coming out. Now you just have to watch. I don't know if you can hear this or not. There it is; multiple shots fired. Secret service and local police are diving after the assailant. There are about two or three people down on the ground. We understand that in addition to the two or three people on the ground, one Secret Service agent and two policemen were also injured. I can't hear the sound on this. I can't hear the sound. We understand that the President and Vice President were both killed. They had just come out of the Washington Hilton. That looks like the President lying face down on the ground on the right and that appears to be the Vice President on the left. All of this happened about five o'clock this evening as the President and Vice President were coming out of the hotel. This is the first time that any of us has seen this. The President, let me repeat, the President *and* the Vice President were both immediately declared dead. This seems to be a shot of the police and Secret Service grabbing the assailant. They're certainly not trying to give any medical assistance to anybody. According to reports he is a young, bald, white male. We will continue to bring you more as details become available."

Traci slept restlessly all night, as she tossed and turned. When she woke up in the middle of the night, Bill was standing at the window, in the dark. She got out of bed and stood behind him, her chin resting on his shoulder.

"Can't sleep?" she asked.

"Not really. I've been thinking about something you said tonight. Do you really believe I don't consider you an equal?"

"Bill, I may not always live in your world, but I do understand how it works. If I were white your mother would be wondering when we'll get married, when we'll have children, and so would everyone else in your life. We've been dating for two years and we live together, but I've never met any of your friends. You never discuss our future. It's as though this relationship has an expiration date. I don't believe that would be the case if I were white."

Bill turned and looked Traci directly in the eyes. "Why would you stay with me if you believe all of this to be true?"

"As much as I hate to admit it, I'm not strong enough to leave. I love you too much."

The silence in the room was deafening. Traci and Bill both realized there was a reason it took two years for them to have such a talk. No other words were spoken for the rest of the night. Bill cradled Traci in his arms and carried her back to bed. They did nothing more than hold one another, clinging together like life rafts. As night fell they slept peacefully in each other's arms.

"Good morning!" Traci beamed.

"Good morning," Bill responded flatly.

"Is everything okay?" Traci asked.

"No, baby, it's not."

"What's wrong?"

"The news is not good."

Traci, like most Americans, assumed that for weeks the news would exclusively be coverage of the President's assassination. However, she didn't anticipate this.

"The Acting President, the former Speaker of the House, has declared a state of emergency. There have been random shootings and lootings throughout the United States. Curfews have been imposed in Boston, New York and Chicago, just to name a few cities."

Snapshots of burned-out stores and people being beaten by the police emblazoned the television screen.

"I don't think you should go into work today," Bill said.

"I can't hide away forever, can I? Can any of us?"

"This will all settle down eventually. The best thing you can do for now is stay put. I understand how committed you are to your kids, but you can't be much help to any of them if you go out there and get hurt."

"I'll be careful."

Bill decided he would get his car out of the garage and drive Traci to work. The moment Bill and Traci left the building they were struck by how surreal it all was. Usually the city block they lived on was bustling with people milling about. Instead, things were deathly quiet. It appeared that many people had decided against braving the unrest that was actively in play.

They walked most of the way to the garage in silence, before Bill spoke.

"It's not so bad down here. There only seem to be one or two stores that were touched."

"One or two is too many," Traci added. "Way too many."

Once in the garage, the attendant seemed surprised to see Bill. "Blue Lexus?" he asked.

"Yeah."

Traci noticed that the attendant seemed to be looking at both her and Bill with contempt. Just when she began to wonder if it was her imagination, he spoke. "Sister, you need to be careful out there. Folks may not be too pleased with certain situations."

"Excuse me?" Traci asked.

"I'm just saying. You look like a nice woman. Folks are mad as hell out here. Somebody might see you and him and take offense."

"Offense to what?" Bill interrupted.

"I was talking to the lady."

"I know you were. I'm just asking a question. Is that still allowed?"

"It's your world. I'm just a squirrel trying to get a nut," the attendant said, sarcastically.

Bill simply smirked and opened the car door for Traci to get in.

Traci watched as the attendant walked away, unsure of whether to be angry with what he had implied or thankful for the warning. For a split second she established eye contact with him and quietly mouthed the words, "Thank you."

Bill got in the car and quickly drove away. "Has everyone gone completely crazy?" he asked Traci.

She said nothing and just shook her head.

As they got closer and closer to the school where Traci taught, it became readily apparent that the school and the surrounding area had not been as lucky as Bill and Traci's neighborhood. There were policemen everywhere and, despite their presence, people were still looting and fighting. The lingering scent of smoke was in the air and as both Bill and Traci looked around, they realized that the level of mayhem that must have ensued after the President was shot had been great. Traci's first thought was of her mother.

CHAPTER TEN

"You're turning into quite the little Liberal, aren't you, son?"

"Mom, come on, you told me you'd try."

"What on earth are you talking about? I'm merely commenting on the subtle little changes that have come about since you met Traci. Taking in that helpless little waif; I didn't know you had it in you."

"Traci is not helpless and if you'll remember, it was Traci that took *me* in."

"I wasn't referring to her. I was talking about her mother."

"Mom, if you continue using these derogatory terms, I'm going to have to insist that you limit your visits."

"What derogatory terms? I simply stated the obvious. Or, maybe I'm wrong? As far as I know she does fit the definition of a stray person; dare I even say, homeless?"

"She's not homeless. She needed a little help. She's getting older and given the current state of things, I didn't think it best for her to be all alone."

"You certainly have no qualms about leaving me alone."

"That is because you are anything but helpless."

"Just you don't forget it, son."

Bill often wondered what his mother's cryptic comments meant. He was well aware of the fact that she could be difficult, but often he was concerned that she was capable of so much more mayhem than he had ever given her credit for. He suddenly remembered that night he had taken his mother and Traci to dinner. Traci was so sure his mother had somehow tainted her food. At first Bill couldn't believe that she was capable of something so heinous. However, it was times like these when he wondered if maybe she was. Both Bill and his mother could hear Traci's voice and that of her mother's as they ascended the stairs.

"Time for me to leave," Mrs. Bianco said.

"Mom, don't be rude. You've never met Traci's mother. Stay put."

"Are you sure you want me to do that?"

The tone in her voice was unmistakable. Bill knew exactly what she was implying.

"I am absolutely sure I want you to stay. I not only want you to stay, I also want you to be nice."

Mrs. Bianco chuckled.

"I'm not kidding, Mom."

"You don't appear to be. Don't worry, darling. I'll be on my very best behavior."

Traci's mother looked different than she did the first time Bill had met her. She seemed a bit disheveled and the feisty, energetic spirit she possessed when he had met her several months earlier appeared to be gone.

"Hello, Mrs. Sanders."

"Hello, Bill and please call me Bertha. I'm so sorry to intrude on you and Traci, but my daughter is so stubborn. She refused to take no for an answer. I keep trying to tell her I'm fine. I'm just fine."

"Mom, you're not fine. Your apartment was like an icebox and there was nothing in your fridge."

"I like it a little cool and I don't eat as much as I used to."

Bill and Traci exchanged looks. It was clear there was something more going on with Traci's mother.

"Oh, Bertha, I'd like you to meet my mother, Candace Bianco."

Bill's mother removed a pair of leather gloves from her pocket and put them on. After she was finished, she shook Bertha Sander's hand.

Traci was boiling mad but did her best to conceal her anger. She knew what the gesture was about. Instead, she looked Bill directly in the eyes and forced him to acknowledge his mother's insulting behavior.

"It's very nice to meet you, Mrs. Sanders. So, you're the mother of this enchanting young woman who has stolen my Bill's heart."

"Nice to meet you too, Mrs. Bianco."

"Well, I'm going to have to leave you fine people."

Mrs. Bianco reached over and air kissed Bill.

"Mom, are you going to be okay getting home?"

"Of course; the driver is waiting for me outside. Good-bye, Mrs. Sanders, Traci."

Traci didn't think she had ever met anyone that brought out the worst in her more than Candace Bianco. She suddenly had the overwhelming urge to trip the little bitch up or maybe even knock her down the stairs.

"So, Mrs. Sanders, I mean Bertha, are you hungry at all?"

"I'm just fine. Please don't fuss over me. I'll be out of your hair before you know it. In the meantime, act like I'm not here. Besides, instead of worrying about me, we should be checking on Darren. I don't know what possessed that boy to move to Mississippi of all places."

"You're not in our hair at all. It's a pleasure to have you here and we can call Darren if you're concerned, even though I'm sure he's fine," Bill said.

"Mama, see, I told you; even Bill says Darren's probably okay. You worry too much." Traci locked eyes with Bill and sent him a knowing look. "You can take the bedroom. Bill and I will sleep on the futon."

"Those things are the worst for your back. Why don't you let me sleep on the futon? I already have a bad back, it won't make much of a difference one way or another. You two have got to go to work and all. You need to get a good night's sleep."

"From what I hear, you've been working, too," Traci said.

"What you talking about, girl?" Traci's mother asked.

"Mama, I know what you've been doing? I spoke to Mae and she told me you've been mopping the halls in the buildings and disposing of the garbage outside. Why are you doing that? I told you I'd take care of things."

"That Mae Whitman's got a big mouth. I swear she can't hold water. Don't make trouble, Traci. It's fine. A little bit of work never killed nobody."

"Mama, you've done more than your share of work. That's why you're retired. You're getting older and that kind of work is much too hard."

"It's easier to just do it."

"What do you mean?"

"One of the women on the ninth floor refused to do it and she got an apartment full of mice because of it."

"What are you talking about? That doesn't make any sense. What do you mean, she got an apartment full of mice? Do you mean the building refused to exterminate?"

"No, just what I said. She got an apartment full of mice. Somebody planted them there. It's been like that all over the complex. People complain or, for the older folks, their kids complain, and then things happen. Suddenly, there's an abundance of roaches, mice or even worse, rats. There have been leaks and apartment flooding and one woman fell while crossing the roof. Or, at least we're hoping all she did was fall."

"What do you mean, hoping? You're not trying to say someone pushed her, are you?"

"Her son made much more trouble than most. She was on the last floor and so when the elevator was out, she would go to the other building and cross the roof to get to her building, so she wouldn't have to walk the fourteen flights up. There's solid flooring between each building, so it's anybody's guess how she fell, unless she was leaning over the edge or someone threw her over the edge."

Traci wasn't sure if she should attribute what she had heard to the ravings of a woman getting up in age or if there really was something highly suspect going on.

"Just don't make waves, baby. Your mother is stronger than she looks. I'll be fine."

In the weeks that followed Traci made every effort to make contact with Darren, to no avail.

"Bill, I think something's wrong with Darren. I've called him several times and left messages every time and still nothing. It's not like him. Have you heard anything on the news about Mississippi?"

"Baby, things are strained all over. You see how it's been here. We all expected things to return to normal within a couple of days, yet people are still fighting mad. The President's assassination was bad enough, but to have a Republican sworn in as acting President. There are rumors circulating that it was the Republicans that assassinated The President. To swear the present Speaker of the House in as President, even if he was next in line in the succession, was a dangerous gamble. The *powers that be* had to know there would be some backlash."

"Well, if I don't hear from Darren soon, I'm going down there."

"Traci, are you sure that's a good idea? I don't think now is the best time for a trip to the Deep South."

"It doesn't matter where it is, that's where my brother is and if

I can't reach him by phone, I'm going right down to Mississippi and get him."

"When do we leave?" her mother asked.

"Shit!" Traci cursed under her breath.

This was one of those times the fact that her mother was hard of hearing made things much easier. Although, she somehow still seemed to hear exactly what she didn't want her to hear.

"What did you say, Mom?"

"You know exactly what I said, Missy. If you're going down to Greenville to bring my boy back, I'm going with you."

"Mama, I was just talking. Neither of us can go down to Mississippi now. I'm sure Darren will call us in a day or two. It might just be that his phone is broke. You know how often he does that."

Darren didn't call the next day or the day after that. In fact, it was weeks before Traci or her mother heard anything from him at all.

"In an effort to get her mother to stop threatening to head down to Mississippi to get Darren, Traci lied and told her she had spoken to Darren and he was fine. With her concern about Darren under control, Traci's mother relaxed a little and soon became less and less interested in returning home. It was trying, having her mother and Bill in such a small apartment, but after stopping off one day to pick up some things from her mother's apartment, she had no intention of letting her go back to that place.

Traci knew something was wrong the moment she walked in. Her mother had always been meticulous about the way her home was kept. Yet, her place looked as though it had been struck by a cyclone. All of her things were scattered about and Traci was sure the sounds she was hearing were the pitter-patter of tiny little rodent claws. She grabbed an armful of clothes and was about to leave when an envelope fell to the floor. It was from the Department of Housing. Traci felt a bit uncomfortable about reading her mother's mail, but realized that it was important that she have a clear picture of her mother's circumstances. She opened the letter and read it.

Dear Mrs. Sanders,

It has come to our attention that you have not satisfied the requirements of your housing project work program. As stated in earlier correspondence to you, any tenant found to be negligent in their assigned duties will be evicted based on the housing projects rules and obligations. I understand that you have been a tenant for the past 35 years and therefore, we would prefer not to take the steps necessary to separate you from your home. Unfortunately, said steps will be necessary if you continue to willfully disregard these notices, and more specifically, your obligations.

Sincerely Yours,

Housing Project President

Traci couldn't believe she had been so removed from things that she hadn't seen this coming. For years there had been talk of tenants in housing projects eventually being forced to care for the residences they lived in. Somehow, though, like so many others, Traci had assumed that would include tenants on public assistance and younger people with no real tangible obligations. When rumblings of the possibility first began, Traci assumed even women with small children would be exempt. The word complacency kept springing to her mind. Complacency had been what created these circumstances. It was even complacency that had killed the President.

Suddenly Traci was nervous and uncomfortable about being in

the apartment. She grabbed a stack of clothing in her arms and didn't even take the time to find something to put it in. She was thankful she had listened to Bill and taken the car. She rushed out of the apartment, jumped in the driver's seat and drove away. As she pulled away, she saw several tenants bagging leaves and garbage outside the various buildings of the complex.

She cried all the way home. She didn't know for sure why she was crying, except for the overpowering feeling of doom that filled her.

CHAPTER ELEVEN

"I've been thinking maybe we should consider getting a bigger place, something outside of the city," Bill said.

"Where's this coming from?" Traci asked.

"This place is too small for the three of us and I would like for your mom to be more comfortable. She can't keep sleeping on that futon thing. Besides, if the need should arise for your brother to return to New York and he needs a place to stay, it will be a lot easier with more room."

"Were you considering buying a place or renting something? Can we afford to buy something right now? You know my job is iffy at best."

"We should probably buy something. Don't worry about the money. The security business is booming. We have a lot of huge clients and the company is growing every day."

"It's funny; although you may not find this so funny, but if it wasn't for Eleanor, Satellite Security would be in a lot of trouble right now. She secured a huge account right before you and I moved in together."

"Ole Eleanor. How is the Ice Queen anyway?"

"So, I was thinking Long Island or maybe New Jersey. What do you think?" Bill said, attempting to change the subject.

"It wasn't so long ago I thought I hated the burbs, but it's funny how things can change. I could get used to domestic bliss with you."

"I can't promise domestic bliss, but I can promise to love, honor, comfort and cherish you from this day forward, forsaking all others and keeping only unto you, for as long as we both shall live."

Mrs. Sanders couldn't conceal her excitement at what she hoped was a marriage proposal Bill was making to her daughter.

"Girl, you better say yes."

"Huh?"

"Your mother is right. You better say yes."

A grin slowly spread across Traci's face and she jumped up squealing and clutching Bill around his neck, when the realization of what he was saying hit.

"I do! I do! I do!" she screamed.

Suddenly the smile disappeared and Traci was serious.

"Have you told your mother yet?" she asked.

"Can we navigate one hurdle at a time please?"

"No problem, Mr. Bianco."

"No problem, Future Mrs. Bianco."

Traci was nervous about what Bill's mother would say but she did like the sound of it—Mrs. Traci Sanders Bianco. It had a nice ring to it.

While Traci and her mother talked about what kind of wedding they would have, Bill went into the bedroom to call his mother.

"We have to talk," he said.

"Fire away," his mother responded on the other end of the line.

"You don't exactly feel warm and fuzzy about Traci and the life I've chosen for myself, but I've asked her to marry me."

"I assumed that would be coming soon."

Bill was surprised at how calm she was. "Did you really?"

"Of course I did. You forget; I was young once. A man doesn't invite his girlfriend's mother to live with them unless he has plans of making things quite permanent."

"What are your thoughts?" Bill asked.

"Bill, darling, why do you ask me questions that you really don't want to know the answer to? I will say that you should be very sure that you are prepared for what will inevitably come."

"What does that mean?"

"It means that our world hasn't changed all that much. As quiet as it is kept, differences are not as greatly celebrated as much of society would like to have us believe. Are you fully prepared for what will come?"

"I was prepared from the very first day I met her. I've never felt this way about anyone in my entire life. I love her, Mom. I really and truly do love her. I would do anything for her. She's already proven that she would do anything for me. She saved me and if I have to spend the rest of my life, I will do everything I can to return the favor."

"You do know my participation will be limited. I'll be at the wedding if you would like, but that's as far as it will go."

"I understand."

"So, when is the big day?"

"I would like to do it as soon as possible, but I know how women are with weddings. Traci may want to do something big. We'll figure things out. She can have whatever she wants."

"Well, keep me posted. I'd like to know the date as soon as possible, so I can check my calendar."

"I will. And, Mom, thank you."

"For what? I didn't do anything."

"I was so worried about your reaction."

"You are a grown man and I learned a long time ago when it comes to matters of love and sex you can't tell any man what to do and who to want. Your father taught me that."

Bill and his mother said good-bye and after hanging up the phone,

Candace Bianco couldn't help but marvel at how, no matter how hard you tried to alter destiny, somehow history still repeated itself.

Mention of his father reminded Bill of what kind of husband and father he swore he would never be. It was his firm belief that the man that his father was is what turned his mother into the woman that she was; angry, distrustful and, on occasion, downright mean. His father had spent most of his marriage to his mother openly cheating on her with an endless string of women. He not only cheated, but he was horrible about it. He would flaunt other women in his mother's face as if she deserved to be hurt. Bill never stopped hating his father, even after he died. He often wondered why his mother never left. It was his assumption that it was because of the money, but given his father's cheating, she would have been able to get whatever she wanted.

Bill's father told the story often—at dinner parties, while playing golf; anyplace where he had a captive audience. He would explain to them how he started with one small security company and built his business into a multi-million dollar empire. Every time he would start talking about it, his mother would get that "I wish he would shut up" look on her face.

What Bill remembered were the fights that would follow his father's story telling.

"Must you always talk about money?" she would say.

"You don't want me to talk about it, but you certainly have no problem spending it," his father often said.

"Richard Bianco, you had no class when I married you and you still have no class."

"Oh, as if you had so many better offers."

"My friends don't want to hear you brag about how much money you've got. You know what they say, people that are used to having money never talk about it."

"I supposed you're referring to your blue-blooded parents."

"They're one example."

"Yeah, that was a real class act they pulled, getting rid of you. How horrible does a daughter have to be for her own parents not to stomach her? I may not have much class, but at least my parents liked me."

"I've listened to you tell that same boring story for years and that would be bad enough. But, the story isn't even the truth. If it weren't for my father, you wouldn't have even had that company. Your parents certainly didn't have anything. If it weren't for my father, you'd be a car mechanic."

Bill remembered his mother laughing loudly.

"A grease monkey, that's what you'd be; a lame-brain, grease monkey."

"Stop laughing at me!" The angrier he got, the more his mother would laugh. "I said stop it!"

His mother would taunt him until his father would often strike her. Bill remembered wanting to defend his mother but being too afraid to intervene.

"Whenever you tell that story, you talk about how you built your empire, but not once have I heard you mention that my father gave you your start. He built it and you followed behind like a lap dog. It would have taken a retard to fuck it up, but you're trying to convince everybody that you're some kind of captain of industry. Right! The only thing you're captain of is sterility."

Bill remembered the day his mother said the word *sterility*. He didn't understand what it meant and after he heard the word, and saw the effect it had on his father, he had to know what it meant. They always kept a large Merriam-Webster dictionary in the house. Bill opened it up and tried to sound out the word. When he read the definition: *inability to produce offspring*, he was even more confused.

It wasn't too long after that that his father started spending time with a lot of different women. He would come in late and, according to his mother, would be reeking of cheap perfume. His household was certainly not a happy-go-lucky one.

Bill sat on the edge of the bed, listening to Traci and her mother chatter happily about their plans for the wedding. He considered going into the living room and telling Traci about his conversation with his mother to set her mind at ease. Instead, he got lost in thoughts of his last days with his father. Memories of the day his father died came flooding back.

Bill was only twelve years old when his father passed away, but he remembered every detail of that day as if it were yesterday. He often watched Robert Bianco from a distance, careful not to alert him of his presence.

"Bring him to me," his father had said.

"Why?" he remembered his mother asking.

"Because I'm still the head of this household and I want to see him. Right now, Candace. Don't you dare challenge me because I'm on my death bed."

Bill remembered how nervous his mother looked that day. She was more agitated than he had ever seen her.

"Your father wants to see you."

Bill was terrified of the elder Bianco and when he first learned that his father was dying, he often prayed that he would pass away silently in the night.

He stood in the doorway waiting. Still as ornery as ever, even with all those tubes and oxygen hooked to him, he yelled at Bill.

"What are you, stupid or something? Why are you standing all the way over there? Come closer."

Bill slowly crossed the room, hoping that his father wouldn't use this last opportunity with the two of them together to strike him. That was how Bill spent most of his waking moments, believing that his father was going to hit him. Though he never had, it always seemed as though he was on the verge of doing so. Words spoken to Bill were always in anger and contempt and Bill had resigned himself to knowing that his father never loved him.

"I have something to tell you," his father said. He grinned and it was like looking at a gruesome skeleton. "I've been waiting to tell you this for twelve long years. You're…"

Bill listened alertly, waiting to hear what his father had to say. As he waited, he never lost sight of his mother's face. He always looked to her to lighten the load of whatever encounter he had with his father and this day was no different. For so many years, his mother seemed able to withstand anything his father tossed her way, including protecting Bill and making up for the love and affection his father never provided. She never seemed daunted by any of it, at all. Even when Bill was his most needy, somehow, his mother seemed untouched by it all. She was his rock. Standing by his father's bedside waiting for him to die and waiting to hear what it was he had to say, was the first time he sensed alarm from his mother. All the color drained from her face and she couldn't look Bill in the eye.

"Come closer, boy! What are you looking at her for?"

Just as Bill leaned in to hear what his father had to say, the elder Bianco began coughing. He seemed unable to catch his breath and his mother rushed over. From her jacket pocket she withdrew a syringe. She injected Robert Bianco with the contents and he immediately stopped coughing. Within seconds he drifted off into what appeared to be a restful sleep. It was not.

"Mom, is he…?" Bill asked.

"Yes, honey, he is."

Bill had always been a good child. He was an altar boy and a source of pride to his mother. That was why he felt an over-whelming sense of guilt at the joy he felt when it was confirmed that his father was finally dead. As if reading his thoughts, his mother reassured him.

"Bill, you don't have to feel bad about what you're thinking right now. It's understandable. You and your father never really got along. I want you to understand that it wasn't you he disliked. It was me. He didn't like me and because of that you had to suffer; and for that I am sorry. I promise you I will make things better for you. No one will ever hurt you again, ever."

Bill was sure that his mother's comments were simply to make him feel better. His father had to hate him. Otherwise, why would he have treated him the way that he had?

Bill curled up on the bed and slept, trying to block memories of his father and his early life from his mind. He tried to think of Traci and their new life. More than anything, he wanted to break the cycle. He wanted their marriage to bear no resemblance to that of his mother and father. He wanted their children to feel nothing but love from both parents.

Bill was awakened by Traci's gentle touch, sometime around 10:00 p.m.

"Baby, you were sleeping so peacefully, I didn't have the heart to wake you. You didn't eat anything. Aren't you hungry?"

"All I need is you," he whispered.

He wrapped his arms around her and slept as close to her as he could all night.

Even with all the planning for the wedding, Traci couldn't help but worry about Darren. After leaving even more voicemail messages, he finally called late at night.

"Hey, baby girl."

"Oh my God! Darren, are you okay?"

"I'm fine, baby girl. I'm fine."

"Mom and I have been so worried about you. I tried calling your job yesterday and they said you no longer work there. What's going on?"

"It's the same old revolution, just a different time period."

"Darren, you're not making any sense."

"I know, but I will. I listened to your messages, but the last one you left is the reason I called so late. You're getting married?"

"Yes, and I want you to walk me down the aisle."

"Traci, I can't talk now, but I'm going to call you tomorrow. Okay?"

"Okay? Darren, you're scaring me."

"You know typically that would be the last thing I would want to do, but right now, we all *need* to be scared. I'll call you tomorrow. And, Traci, be careful."

Before Traci could ask Darren what he meant, the phone went dead.

CHAPTER TWELVE

*T*raci's phone rang while she was being fitted for her wedding dress. Traci and Sandra had become good friends and she couldn't think of anyone she would rather have as her maid-of-honor. The fact that Sandra was always on the ball was also a plus. Traci understood why she was the school principal. Even now, she was navigating the waters between Traci and her mother; running interference when Traci was too overwhelmed to deal with caring for her mother, planning a wedding, working as a teacher and house-hunting. As soon as the phone rang, Sandra handed it to Traci before her mother could get to it. When Traci saw the area code, she was glad that she had.

"I'll be right back," Traci said.

"Where are you going?" her mother asked.

"It's one of the parents from school. She's a little hard of hearing and I don't want to disturb the other brides with my screaming," she lied. As soon as Traci was out of her mother's earshot she spoke. "Darren, is that you?"

"Yes, Traci. I'm in the airport, in Greenville."

"Really!" Traci squealed excitedly.

"Yeah; my flight gets into LaGuardia around four."

"Why didn't you call me sooner? Bill and I could have picked you up."

"I want to talk to you alone first. Can you meet me somewhere? Can you meet me at the airport?"

"Sure. Of course I can. I'll get the car."

"Where are you now?" Darren asked.

"I'm in Manhattan. I'm being fitted for my wedding dress."

"Is Bill or Mom there?"

"Really, Darren, why would Bill be here for my fitting? What kind of a gay man are you? You know that it's bad luck for the groom to see the bride in her dress before the wedding."

Traci didn't miss the fact that the joke elicited no response from Darren.

"Who is with you?" he asked.

"Mom and Sandra are with me."

"Who is Sandra?"

"I told you about her. She's the principal at my school. She's the one I wanted you to meet. She's militant, too," Traci added, jokingly.

"Only get the car if you can do it without telling Bill. Otherwise, I can meet you in Manhattan. Don't bring Mom or Sandra."

"Okay, Darren. Why the cloak and dagger routine?"

"I'll explain everything when I see you this afternoon."

Traci hung up and returned to her mother and Sandra. She hoped neither of them would notice her change in mood. She tried her best to camouflage her worry, but it was difficult. There was definitely something wrong and, glancing at her watch, she realized she would have to wait at least five hours before she found out what. She continued with her fitting. However, the last thing on her mind was a dress. While Traci's mother talked to the store proprietor about the wedding dress, Traci pulled Sandra off to the side.

"Sandra, I wanted to thank you for running interference with my cell phone and my mother. She's my mother and I love her, but she still thinks I'm a kid and therefore undeserving of privacy. As soon as that phone rings, she's got it in hand, looking at the number to see who is calling."

"She's probably hoping it's your brother."

"How'd you know about Darren?"

"Your mother mentioned to me that she hadn't spoken to him in a while. She's a little worried. Has your brother mentioned any of what's happening down in Mississippi?"

"No, he hasn't. That was him on the phone just now. He didn't seem to want to talk to my mom. That's why I didn't say anything. He's getting on a flight today to come to New York. He wants me to meet him. There's something he wants to talk to me about that he wanted to do in private. What's happening in Mississippi?"

"I'll let him talk to you about the specifics, but that little bit of looting and rioting here in New York was the tip of the iceberg. Things are crazy down South. The scary thing is, it's like everything is purposely being kept hush-hush. It frightens me to think who or what has that kind of power."

Traci was more confused than before. She realized how little attention she had been paying to current events. She was so wrapped up in Bill, her mother and the wedding that she had been neglecting the rest of the world. She decided before she even met with Darren she would do her own digging and figure out what was going on in his corner of the U.S. After leaving the dress shop, she said good-bye to Sandra, went home with her mother and left the apartment shortly after. While she was waiting for the garage attendant to get the car, she pulled out her android and turned it on. As soon as she typed in Mississippi, it was apparent that Darren did indeed have a good deal to be concerned about.

One story talked about a protest at the University of Mississippi against the re-election of the President. According to the story, the protest that started with only forty or so students in the student union grew into a crowd of more than four hundred people after rumors of a riot spread on social media. Many of those in attendance were shouting racial slurs and using profanity. Traci was disconcerted to learn a little known fact mentioned in the article she was completely unaware of. Apparently, the university was the scene of violent rioting in 1962, when integration was forced and its first black student, James Meredith, enrolled at the school. The further she read the more stories she found ones where gay men and some women were beaten and killed. It seemed rampant. Traci wondered if the large numbers of hate crimes was a more recent occurrence or if she was so removed from it all that she was just becoming aware of the problem. The more she searched the worse it seemed to get. Then, she stumbled upon a blog that she hoped was nothing more than wild speculation and rumors. It talked about the President's desire to overturn the 1967 U.S. Supreme Court decision that deemed anti-miscegenation laws unconstitutional.

On and on she read, still ashamed of her lack of awareness. The title of one article in particular read, Interracial Marriage: *Many Deep South Republican Voters Believe Interracial Marriage Should be Illegal.* There were stories of couples banned from churches, employees fired and worse still, people beaten and even killed, simply because they married someone of a different ethnic background. Many of the stories were old, but the occurrences seemed to be increasing in greater numbers and severity since the President and the Vice President were killed.

She was so distracted, she barely noticed the attendant get out of the car and walk up behind her.

"Interesting reading," he said.

Traci wasn't sure if it was the content of what she was reading or the surprise of seeing the attendant standing so close to her, but she jumped.

"I'm sorry," she said. "You scared me."

"No need to be scared, at least not of me. Now those stories you're reading, those you should be very scared of."

"I can't believe this is the first time I read any of this."

"It's not so surprising. Many of us, especially in cities like this, have settled into a comfortable complacency."

Traci was struck by the fact that shame seemed to be the order of the day for her. She was struck by the garage attendant's intelligence and realized she had assumed he would not be capable of such thoughts merely because of the job he held.

"I guess I fall into that category as well."

"Don't be ashamed. It's understandable. Most of us don't question many of the world's inequalities until we're directly affected by them. The more financially and socially comfortable we are, the less involved we are. You'd be surprised how few people really and truly get involved in the issues that affect our world." He paused and looked at her. "How are you and that young man you're dating doing?"

"We're okay, I guess. We're supposed to be getting married next month. After reading this, I have a better understanding of your warning during the riots."

Traci was surprised to hear herself say the words *supposed to be getting married*. In just a few short hours and after reading some articles, she was already questioning her marriage to Bill.

"Yeah, I have family in the South," the attendant mentioned. "I know what it was like the week the President was killed. The stuff that was going on here was nothing compared to the Southern States."

"Stuff like this couldn't really happen, could it? It can't be that easy to overturn a Supreme Court decision, like the one legalizing interracial marriage."

"You'd be surprised at how easy it could be."

"Really, but how? There would be rioting in the streets."

"You mean like we had recently; the same rioting that lasted a few days here and eventually died down?"

"Point taken," Traci agreed.

"You know, we've been standing here talking for almost ten minutes and I see you with your fiancé all the time and I don't know your name."

"Hi, I'm sorry. My name is Traci; Traci Sanders."

"I'm Omar. It's nice to meet you, Traci."

"Same here."

"For years I've listened to black folks talk about what they would have done if they were slaves. How they would have fought and why that could never happen again because of our strength and unity. As quiet as it's kept, it required a black president to even get most of us out there to vote. Before his nomination, how many people of color *really* went out there and cast their votes in any political election? It's only been fifty-three years since the Voting Rights Act was enacted, yet many of us still don't vote. It's a damn shame. When my sons are screwing up in school, I always remind them that it wasn't so long ago that they would have been beaten or even killed if they dared to pick up a book. We consider ourselves free men, but freedom is more than the physical structure that houses us or the amount of money in our pockets. Freedom is a state of mind."

Traci realized she was one of those people he was talking about. She wasn't truly free. She, like so many others, took way too much for granted.

"Oh, and to answer your earlier question, Traci; there are countless ways that even overturning a Supreme Court decision could be accomplished. There are legitimate ways and illegitimate ways. I won't even mention the legitimate ones, because I'm convinced that when it happens there isn't going to be a thing legitimate about it."

"In your opinion, what are the illegitimate ways?"

"Well, little lady, there are a few. When it comes to the Supreme Court, the Executive Branch can obstruct a decision or even fail to enforce it. Or, Congress can rewrite legislation to bring it into compliance with constitutional guidelines. Congress even has the power to strip the Supreme Court of its appellate jurisdiction over some cases, seizing their ability to overturn laws and policy. As if that isn't enough, individual states sometimes pass laws that obviously violate Supreme Court decisions; in doing that they can force someone with standing to challenge the new law's constitutionality. In the meantime those same laws can be enforced whether it violates our civil rights or not. State legislatures do this to overturn or slip around precedents set by earlier Courts. It's passive resistance at its finest. Only problem is it's usually not so fine for people of color."

"It was great talking to you, Omar. I hope we can continue this at some other time. I feel like I've learned so much in so little time."

"I'm here. Feel free to pick my brain anytime."

Traci got into Bill's car and headed to the airport. Traffic was bumper to bumper and after she had been on the road for about a half-hour, her cell phone rang. It was Bill. She considered not answering it, but decided it was best that she answer.

"Hey," she said.

"Is everything okay?" Bill asked.

"Yeah; everything's fine. Why do you ask?"

"I stopped by the garage to pick up the car and they mentioned that you had picked it up."

"You said I could use it anytime, right?"

"Oh, yeah, of course; that's why I added your name at the garage. I was just concerned because you hadn't mentioned that you were going to use it."

"It was a last-minute thing. There were some dresses I wanted to look at in Queens and I didn't figure that out until my fitting today," she lied.

"Oh. Do you want me to cook dinner tonight or should we go out?"

"It doesn't matter to me. Either one is good."

"You sure you're okay, Traci?"

"Of course, I'm fine. Everything's fine."

"That's a lot of fines," Bill joked.

Traci laughed.

"That's better. I'll see you when you get home. Have fun shopping."

"I will. See you later."

"See you later."

Traci couldn't help but think about how easily a person's life could be altered in a very short period of time. When she got up that morning, her biggest challenge was whether or not she was going to wear a veil at her wedding. Now, she was contemplating whether or not it was wise to even have a wedding.

CHAPTER THIRTEEN

*T*raci was happy that she had arrived before Darren's flight got in. She wanted to meet him at the gate, so she parked the car and made her way to the arrivals area of the airport. While she was waiting she continued perusing the Internet. She Googled some of the information Omar had shared with her and was blown away by the fact that everything he said was absolutely true. She was impressed with the wealth of information he was able to provide and genuinely hoped they would have an opportunity to talk again.

When it was time for Darren's flight to get in, Traci stood up and made her way to the optimum spot for him to see her. She was shocked when she saw him. Darren, who was usually the best-dressed man in the room, looked disheveled and instead of his usual youthful appearance he seemed worn out and as if he had aged ten years. He smiled broadly as soon as he caught sight of her and the brother she remembered seemed to return.

"Hey, baby girl," he said, grabbing her and holding on tightly.

"Hey, you!"

Traci declined to mention his appearance. The last thing she wanted to do was make him feel uncomfortable. It was obvious whatever was going on with him in Mississippi, he had been through enough.

"Where are your bags?"

"This is it."

"That's all you brought? How long are you staying?"

"I'm not sure yet. Let's get out of this airport and we'll talk about it."

Once in the car, Traci felt as though she could speak much more freely.

"Darren, what's been going on with you in Greenville? I didn't want to say anything earlier, but you look so tired. You're not sick, are you?"

"No, it's nothing like that. Shit has been rough. I told you I joined that group right."

"Yeah, you mentioned it; the COC, right?"

"Yeah, that's it."

"Bryan's a member, too, isn't he?" Traci asked.

"Yeah, he is. Some things never change, though. Just like it was in the sixteen- and seventeen-hundreds, the South is in much worse shape than up here in the North. The group has chapters all over the United States and all kinds of members. A lot of the information we get comes from those who are politically connected. When some of the information first started to materialize, even I was skeptical, but after the Empire State Building went down I started to realize that a lot of what was circulating and many believed were rumors, was in fact the real deal. That's why I'm here now."

"Really? Tell me, Darren, what's going on?"

"Do you know anything about Bill's business dealings?"

"Bill?"

"Yes, Bill."

"He doesn't talk about his business all that much. It's a family business and his mother was the CEO before Bill took over."

"Did you know that the company that Bill owns handles the security for the Empire State Building?"

"Are you sure? Bill would have mentioned that if they did."

"I'm quite sure. I wouldn't tell you any of this if I hadn't researched all of it first. It's all a matter of public record. In fact, I sort of stumbled on the fact that it was Bill's company. That name is pretty damned distinguishable, after all."

"Darren, are you absolutely sure?"

Darren began digging around in one of the two bags he arrived with. "Take a look at this."

"Let's get out of here. I'll look at that when we get home."

"I'm not sure I want to do that yet," Darren mentioned.

"Darren, Mom has been worried sick about you, even though she tries not to let on. You can't come all the way to New York and not see her."

"And just how do I explain this," he said, pointing to the scars on his face.

Traci touched his face.

"How did that happen?"

"Which one?"

"Are you telling me that this happened more than once?"

"Unfortunately, yes. The first time I thought it was a simple, run-of-the-mill gay bashing, but it didn't take me long to figure out it was more than that. This country is headed for trouble and people like you and I are smack dab in the middle of it. We are going to fare the worst. The corrupt politicians, the hate mongers and the racists have to be stopped. Otherwise, we're doomed."

"Darren, what you're trying to do with this organization is admirable, but what are you going to do, let your convictions and beliefs kill you?"

"I'd rather die a free man than live as an enslaved one."

"That is some straight up bullshit, Darren. This has got to stop! I won't sit by and watch you get wrapped up in something you obviously can't handle. You're only one man."

"See, that's the attitude that put us exactly where we are now. That's what the COC is all about, the power of one man."

"Where was the COC when you were damn near killed?"

"Traci, you don't get it."

"You're right, I don't."

Traci pulled the car out and drove toward the city.

"Can we stop somewhere and get something to eat before we get into Manhattan?"

"Of course."

"Don't look so mad," Darren said, smiling.

"I'm not mad. I'm worried, about you."

"This is bigger than just me, or even you. This is a revolution and if we don't make some headway now, early in the fight, things are going to get much worse."

Traci and Darren noticed a diner before they got into Manhattan and decided to stop and get something to eat.

"Damn, boy, when was the last time you ate?"

"I had some peanuts on the plane and I ate dinner last night."

"Darren, you ain't messin' with no stuff, are you?"

"Drugs? Hell no! I haven't touched that shit since I was in high school."

"I had to ask."

"That's how a lot of people react when they hear what's going on out there. The stuff I've shared with you is the tip of the iceberg. There are members of the COC that are purported to have tangible information pointing to our now President being responsible for our former President and Vice President being assassinated."

"There's one thing I don't understand. If there's all this *tangible* information floating around, why doesn't someone reveal what they have?"

"Come on ,Traci, you're smarter than that. It's not that easy. If everything being said is true, they were able to get past secret service and police and kill not only the President of the United States, but the Vice President as well. Who do you think is gonna reveal that they have that kind of proof? Even I don't know what I would do if I was walking around with that kind of proof. I'd like to think that I would step up to the plate, but quite frankly, I don't know. It's a scary position to be in."

"I don't know, Darren; it all sounds a bit fantastical to me."

"Let me ask you a question, Traci?"

"What?"

"Since everything that's happened; The President and Vice President being killed, our now Republican President being sworn in, have you heard anything about the President's or the Vice President's wives and children? I mean think about it, when President Kennedy was killed in the sixties, the coverage of his wife and son was non-stop. There have been no photos, no interviews, no images of any kind of either wife."

Traci had to admit, Darren was right. "So, is there a theory about that as well?" she asked.

"Yes, as a matter of fact there is. It is believed that they are either being held captive or were killed."

"But that's got to be easy enough to prove. Why doesn't someone simply ask to see them?"

"Once again, who is going to do that? You? Me?"

While Traci tried to grasp the overwhelming weight of what Darren was trying to tell her, she got quite the shock. Bill walked into the diner toward her and Darren.

"Are you done shopping?" he asked.

"Bill?"

"Forgotten about me already," he said.

"What are you doing here?"

"I was visiting a client and since I missed lunch today, I decided to stop in and get something to eat."

"I thought you said you were heading home when I spoke to you earlier?"

"No, I didn't say that. I asked if you wanted me to cook dinner tonight, but I was still working."

Bill suddenly turned his attention to Darren, extending his hand. "Hello, Bill Bianco," he said, introducing himself.

"I'm Darren, Traci's brother."

"Darren! Boy, is your mother going to be happy to see you. You're all she talks about." He redirected his attention to Traci. "Traci, why didn't you tell me your brother was coming to visit? Wow, this is perfect timing! Traci, I may have found the perfect house. I looked at it today."

"Without me?"

"It was a last-minute thing. One of my clients is selling, so I went by and looked at it. I was going to take you to see it. It's in New Jersey. If we're lucky, maybe we can move quickly. The owner wants to sell it fast. This is great; just in time for Darren's arrival. Darren, I mentioned to Traci how nice it would be to have a place big enough where you can stay if you decide to come back to New York."

"I'm just visiting, man," Darren said.

"Oh. I thought you might want to get out of Mississippi, with the political climate being what it is in the South right now."

"What do you know about it?" Traci asked.

In all of the conversations they had had about Darren, Traci didn't ever remember Bill mentioning *the political climate in the*

South. In fact, most of the time he seemed mostly disinterested and she assumed he only listened out of love for her.

Ignoring Traci's question, Bill looked directly at Darren. "Shall we all go home? Your mother will be very happy to see you, Darren."

CHAPTER FOURTEEN

As Traci, Bill and Darren were leaving the diner, Traci's phone rang.

"Hey Sandra; thanks for... What!" Bill and Darren both stared at Traci. "How? Where is she?"

"What is it?" Darren asked in a panic.

"Darren, Mom's in the hospital. She's got pneumonia. I didn't get a chance to tell you yet, but she wasn't in great shape, so I brought her to live with Bill and me. She's been fine since she's been living with us, but I don't know. Maybe she had some sort of a relapse. Sandra picked her up so they could go and do one of the registries and she passed out in the store. Sandra took her to Beth Israel."

"Why didn't you tell me?" Darren asked.

"I didn't have a chance. We were so busy talking about that other stuff we didn't get to Mom and what's been going on with her."

"Yeah, I know," Darren said, staring at Bill. Bill refused to engage Darren and simply looked away. "Mom is usually very healthy. How did she get so sick?"

"Well, Mom isn't getting any younger and the work she was doing in that building didn't help any. She was probably doing too much."

"What work around the building?"

"Remember the letter I told you she received?"

"Not that letter from the housing project enforcing that work for shelter program?"

"Yes."

"Traci, I thought you were going to take care of that?"

"I tried to, but Mom wanted me to stay out of it. Not only that, the City or whoever manages the project building has been strong-arming the tenants. You know most of the people who live in Mom's building are elderly. The stories Mom told me about what they were doing to tenants who didn't do their share were horrendous. I went over there to get some of her things right after she came to stay with us and Mom's place looked like it had been ransacked, or maybe she was so tired from working she neglected her housekeeping. You know how meticulous she usually is. The place was a mess. Not only that, as long as the two of us lived there, I don't ever remember there being rodents of any kind. While I was there getting her things I could have sworn I heard some creatures scratching at the floor and walls."

"Thank goodness Sandra was with her," Bill said.

The drive back into the city was mostly silent. Darren kept glancing at Traci. He couldn't wait until they were alone. There was so much more he still wanted to say to her and she hadn't even had an opportunity to look at the papers showing that Bill and his mother owned the company that was in charge of security in the Empire State Building before it was destroyed. He hadn't planned to stay in New York, but now all that had changed. He would have plenty of time to make Traci understand that her marriage to this man was a huge mistake.

"We're here to see Bertha Sanders," Bill said.

"Are you all family?"

"We are," Darren chimed in, motioning to him and Traci.

"This is my fiancé," Traci offered.

Darren's distaste for Bill was immediately obvious to Traci.

She whispered in Darren's ear before they entered their mother's room.

"Darren, Mom likes Bill, so please try to keep your dislike of him to yourself. We don't want to upset her. She's been very active with helping me plan the wedding and she was very excited and happy for me when he proposed. So, be nice. Okay?"

"I won't do anything to jeopardize my mother's health."

"She's my mother too, in case you've forgotten," Traci said.

"The question is whether you've forgotten. You've been so wrapped up in Bill and the wedding. Did you forget that our mother is not a spring chicken and maybe, just maybe, she needed someone to follow-up on that bullshit with the building? Not only that, maybe all this wedding hoopla is too much for her."

"Whatever," Traci said, at a loss for words.

"Yeah, whatever," Darren added, sarcastically.

From behind the two of them Bill chimed in. "Game faces everyone."

"Game faces?"

Somehow Traci was just as annoyed with Bill's cavalier attitude as Darren was.

"Some people will do anything for a free bowl of Jell-O," Darren joked, as he entered his mother's hospital room.

"Oh my God, my baby boy! Darren, how did you get here so quickly?"

"I was going to surprise you. Little did I know you'd be taking a hospital *staycation* when I arrived."

"I've been sick over missing my son. No calls, no visits. What's a mother to do?"

"Well, I'm here now; so get your butt out of that bed and come home."

"Traci and Bill won't let me go home."

"I heard that's with good reason, Ms. Worker Bee. I can't believe my mother is letting them white folks bully her into cleaning some damn floors." Bill's head jerked in Darren's direction. "Present company excepted, of course," Darren lied.

"Darren, honey, behave yourself. Bill, don't you pay him no never mind. I don't know what happened to this boy. He acts like he ain't got no kind of home training. I really did teach him better than this."

"Yeah, yeah, yeah."

"Boy, you better watch your mouth. I don't care how old you are, I'll still swat your behind."

Instead of the visitors making the patient feel better, it was like the patient was lightening the load of the visitors. Even in the midst of all that was going on, everyone managed to be on their best behavior while they were visiting.

The next day Darren and Traci's mother was released from the hospital. She went back to Traci and Bill's apartment, even though it was under protest. Traci convinced Bill to stay home and she and Darren went to the hospital to pick her up. By the time they arrived at the apartment, Bill had prepared a meal fit for a feast, complete with dessert.

Bertha Sanders could smell the food from downstairs.

"I hope that's coming from our place," she said.

"It probably is. Bill likes to cook when he's stressed."

"What's that boy stressed about? You two aren't giving him a hard time are you? Traci? Darren?"

"No, Mama; nobody's giving him a hard time," Traci said.

"That's a good man you got there, Traci. Don't you go and

blow it. And, Darren Emmanuel Sanders, you and I both know you've been jealous and protective of Traci, since ya'll were kids, but that doesn't mean you get to give her future husband a hard time. You hear me?"

"Yes, Mama, I hear you."

"That's good."

"Dag, you're bossy for someone who just got out of the hospital," Darren said sarcastically.

"Don't you know, boy? That's what hospitals are for. They're for old people like me to go and refuel, when life drains our supply."

"Really? Can't say that I've ever heard that one before," said Darren.

"Me neither," Traci agreed.

"See, that's why I'm the mother and ya'll are the children. Mama knows all that important stuff you young whipper snappers don't know a thing about."

"So, what's your story these days, Mr. Sanders? How you gonna go and disappear for weeks and months at a time and forget you got a mother and a sister here who are worried about you?"

Darren was happy they had reached the apartment, so he could avoid his mother's last question. "Traci, I don't think these stairs are a good idea. Look how out of breath she is."

"Would you stop talking about me like I'm not here. I'm in now. I'll rest up for a while and then I'll be good as new."

When they got into the apartment, Bill had the entire spread laid out. He had put out a large folding table with a beautiful tablecloth on it. On the table was an assortment of bread, pasta, cheeses, a large roast, some potatoes and a hearty-looking salad. Traci suddenly became aware of how hungry she was.

"Wow, baby, this looks good."

"I figured you guys would be famished by the time you got back."

"Thanks, Bill. I'm sorry I've been so weird these last couple of days."

"No problem. I've got a mother, too. I understand. I don't know what I would do if my mother was sick. She's like you, Bertha; strong, impenetrable. It's always a shock when someone like that gets sick."

"Did ya'll hear that? Bill thinks I'm impenetrable."

They sat down to the table and ate. Traci assumed her mother was either so happy to be spending time with her son or happy to be out of the hospital, because she hadn't seen her so jovial in a long time. She talked non-stop throughout the evening. While her mother talked, Traci ate so much Darren couldn't resist joking about it.

"I still have my napkin here, if you're still hungry."

Traci turned away from her mother's view and flipped Darren the finger. "Fuck you," she mouthed.

"Such profanity," said Darren.

"Such bullshit," Traci responded.

"Traci, you know it's the strangest thing. While I was in the hospital, I dreamed your friend Sandra had a baby."

"I don't think that's going to happen, Mom."

"Why not? People don't have to be married these days to have a baby."

"It's not her marital status that's the issue. Sandra is a lesbian, Mom."

"That pretty girl? You've got to be kidding."

"So what are you saying? That pretty girls can't be lesbians?"

"Oh stop it. I know pretty girls can be lesbians. It's just surprising, that's all. Anyway, usually a dream like that doesn't mean the person in the dream is pregnant. It usually means someone else. I bet it's you. Did you go and knock my baby up, Bill?"

Bill was speechless. It would have never occurred to him, but it made perfect sense; the weight gain, the moodiness, her ravenous appetite.

"Traci?"

"Why are you all looking at me like I just swallowed a goldfish or something?"

Darren was also staring.

"My God; stop staring at me! Okay, okay. I could be. I don't know. I haven't really been keeping track."

CHAPTER FIFTEEN

With his mother back on the mend, Darren returned to Mississippi, but not before filling Traci in on everything he knew. She seemed to believe him, but Darren could tell the seriousness of the situation was not registering with her.

"Promise me you'll call if you or Mom should need anything."

"I promise."

"Wow! I can't believe I'm going to be somebody's uncle. I like the sound of that—Uncle Darren."

"Me too," Traci agreed. "It's got a nice ring to it."

"One more promise, please, before I leave."

"Yes, Darren, what is it?"

"Promise me that no matter what is going on, you'll do your best to keep your eyes and ears open."

"Of course I will. I'm getting married and having a baby. I'm not brain dead."

"You know that's not what I mean. I just know you've got a lot going on and it's easy to get distracted with other things and miss the big picture."

"I won't. Now it's your turn. You need to promise *me* something."

"Fire away," Darren said.

"Promise me you'll keep Mom and I inside the loop. It's difficult with you being so far away. When you disappeared, we were both scared to death. You have no idea what was going through my head. And, Mom tries to act like she's waiting for you to meet some nice girl and settle down, but she's fully aware of the fact that you're gay and probably was just as worried as I was that you were lying in a ditch somewhere, the victim of gay bashing."

Darren laughed.

"It's not funny, Darren."

"That's not what I'm laughing about. Do you know Mom tried to hook me up with Sandra? Isn't that rich? A gay man and a lesbian? You think if we hooked up, we'd cancel each other out and therefore be able to be considered heterosexual?"

"Only you would say some off-the-wall shit like that."

"You know me."

"Yes, I do; and don't you forget it."

"Don't worry, I won't."

Traci missed Darren after he left but she was anxious to take a nap. She had only been asleep for an hour or so when Bill woke her up.

"What time is it?" she asked.

"It's already three o'clock."

"Bill, I was wondering if maybe we could skip dinner at your mother's today?"

"Traci, it's difficult driving out there every Sunday, but I'm all she's got and she looks forward to these Sunday dinners."

"I don't get it. When we were dating, you only visited her once, maybe twice a month. Now, it's every Sunday."

"Traci, honey, we've been together long enough for you to understand. Despite her overbearing bravado, my mother is painfully insecure and you represent the person that's going to take her son away from her. Until she realizes that's not the case, these Sunday dinners are what she's holding on to."

"I understand, Bill, but it's just I've been so tired and I was hoping to stay in bed all weekend."

"You can rest at my mom's place and we won't stay long. Okay?"

"Okay," Traci conceded.

Traci wasn't really showing yet and was anxious to get married before she was. Unfortunately, Candace Bianco couldn't resist the urge to remind Traci of her growing belly.

"Is it possible that little butterball has gotten even bigger?"

"Mom, really? Traci is not even showing yet."

"So, are you telling me her belly is always like that?"

"No, *her* belly is not always like that," Traci said, referencing herself. "I'm pregnant and my belly is exactly the size it's supposed to be at this stage in my pregnancy. It's barely there."

Traci was ecstatic when dessert came. That meant the evening was drawing to a close.

The next morning Traci was exhausted and moody.

"You want me to call in for you?" Bill asked.

"Why would I want you to do that?"

"That's the third time you hit the snooze button."

"I probably wouldn't be so tired this morning if we hadn't driven all the way out to Jersey to have dinner with your mother."

"Come on, Traci. I don't want to fight. It's too early for that."

Despite Traci's and Bill's urgings, Traci's mother went back to her apartment. She felt like she was in the way and even though Bill tried to encourage her to hang in there until they found the right house, she thought it was best for her to go back to her own place. What Traci realized after her mother left was that she and Bill argued a lot more than they did when her mother was there. She didn't know if it was the pregnancy, the fact that they could be themselves without her mother there, or if it was a backlash of Darren's visit.

"I don't want to fight either, but I wish you and your mother would take into consideration the fact that I'm pregnant, I'm tired and I work a full-time job."

"I've told you time and time again that you don't have to work."

"I want to work. I've never depended on anyone to take care of me in that way and it's not going to start now."

"When are you ever going to learn how to be in a couple?"

Traci was on her feet and out of the bed in record time.

"Excuse me?"

"You heard me. Maybe that's what happened between you and Bryan."

"Fuck you, Bill!"

"That's your answer for everything. You really do act like a spoiled brat sometimes."

"Well, if that isn't the pot calling the kettle black, I don't know what is. You, of all people, have the nerve to call someone a spoiled brat? Is this the same man that goes to have dinner with his mommy every Sunday because he's afraid she'll be angry with him; or is it really that you're afraid she'll tighten the purse strings?"

"Traci, I'm trying my best to be understanding because you're pregnant, but you're trying my patience."

"Yeah, and?"

"You know, your level of dysfunction is unbelievable. You have the nerve to make fun of my closeness with my mom. So, I have dinner with her every Sunday. That's better than completely abandoning your mother in her time of need."

"What are you talking about?"

"Traci, I would never have allowed my mother or her living environment to get to the point that you allowed. How long was your mother living like that before you brought her here? Now she's back in her apartment. Are you going to stay in touch with her now? Will you visit her regularly, or are you going to wait until she's truly incapable of caring for herself?"

"You don't know anything about it. Just because you lived in the same apartment with my mother for a while doesn't make you an expert on who she is. My mother is fiercely independent. She's not like your mother."

Bill went into the bathroom and closed the door. By the time he came back out, she was gone.

Work hadn't gotten any easier for Traci and thanks to an ever-growing increase in budget cuts, Traci's school was even worse off than before she started teaching there. Traci found it hard to believe that things could get any worse for the families in the community, but things did. After a steady decline in the state of the economy, things started to pick up in late 2013. However, positive change was short-lived and by 2015, it became apparent that Americans would have to, once again, begin worrying about the stability of their lives. Shortly on the heels of that realization there was the Presidential assassination and the Empire State Building explosion. People were desperate, crime was on the rise and jobs were not in great supply. With each school budget cut, Traci wondered if she would be next to get the ax, or if, in fact, the school she taught at would be shut down altogether. There were constantly rumblings to that effect. The school was on the list of the worst performing schools in the city. She just didn't know.

"You okay?" Sandra asked Traci.

"I'm fine. Thanks for asking. I guess I am a little tired and I'm worried about my job and what happens to these kids if everyone who cares about them is gone. This community always fares worst in any decline. Many of these kids are already in trouble. What happens if they close this school? I'm not even talking about the obvious, like me losing my job. Where do kids like this go when something like that happens?"

"You worry too much. Everything is going to be fine."

"You think so, huh?"

"Yeah, I do. Now go on and get to class, before those damn kids set the room on fire."

"Sandra! That was not nice."

"It may not have been nice, but it's true."

Traci went rushing down the hall with memories of an exploding container of soda and Mentos candy in her head.

She had been teaching for nearly a half-hour when one of her students ran from the classroom and headed straight for Principal Piper's office. "Ms. Piper, come quick—there's something wrong with Ms. Sanders."

"What?"

"I don't know. She passed out, and there's a whole lot of blood on her chair and the floor."

CHAPTER SIXTEEN

Traci didn't realize how much she wanted a baby until she had a miscarriage. The doctor telling her she was fine and could have other children was of no comfort. While the doctor was speaking she kept thinking, but I wanted *this* baby.

Bill stood near the bed, stroking her head and trying to reassure her. "You hear that, baby? We can try again."

She wanted to say to him, this wasn't a goldfish. A baby can't be replaced that easily. Instead, she stared off into space. Though she begged Bill not to tell her mother what happened, he did. Traci began crying as soon as her mother walked into the hospital room. Sandra, who usually was as strong as nails, couldn't help but cry as well.

"Don't cry, baby. It's fine. You're going to be fine. I spoke to the doctor and it's just one of those things. It's your body's way of telling you there was something wrong. So, you'll try again and the next time, God-willing, you'll have a healthy baby. You're gonna be just fine."

Bertha Sanders sat by her daughter's bedside, singing her a song she hadn't sung since her children were in elementary school. It was from a movie she had seen co-starring Whitney Houston and Denzel Washington, called *The Preacher's Wife*. Though, Mrs. Sanders obviously hadn't had the vocal range of Whitney Houston, she might as well have had to her kids. That song had gotten them through bellyaches, fights with each other and those anxious nights spent waiting for Santa or the Tooth Fairy to arrive. She sung it once again, hoping it would calm her now grownup daughter.

"Mommies and Daddies always believe that their little angels are special indeed and they could grow up to be anything, but who would imagine a King."

It was then that Traci finally went to sleep.

"I knew that would do the trick," Bill said.

"Yeah, at a time like this a girl needs her mother."

"You need a ride home, Mrs. Sanders, Sandra?"

"What did I tell you, child?"

"I'm sorry, *Bertha*, do you need a ride?"

"I'll be fine. I don't have that far to go. Just make sure my daughter is alright."

"We can leave together," Sandra said.

"Don't worry, Bertha. I'll take good care of her," Bill assured her.

The mother of one of Traci's student, a boy named Kevin Smith, stopped by and left Traci a card signed by all the kids. Bill read the card and knew it would make a world of difference to Traci. She always talked about how emotionally distant many of the kids were, how little some of them seemed to care about anyone or anything and the low level of involvement from the parents in the community. He knew the card would buoy her spirits and renew her faith in the impact she had obviously had on her students and their parents.

"She should be awake soon," Bill said.

"I don't want to wake her. Just let her sleep. Hopefully she'll rest through the night. When do you think she'll be going home?"

"If I were going to guess, I would say tomorrow.

"Yeah, these hospitals these days wanna push you out as soon as possible. You should probably try to get some sleep yourself. She's going to need you tomorrow."

"Point taken."

"Good. Please contact the school and let us know if Ms. Sanders needs anything. All the kids love her, especially my son."

"I will."

Bill couldn't bear to leave Traci alone in a hospital room overnight. He resolved to sit it out until someone kicked him out. When the clock read 2:00 a.m., he decided to make himself comfortable. He pulled a second chair under his legs and reclined as comfortably as he could.

"Good morning, Mr. Bianco. Your wife is being released today."

"I'm not his wife yet," Traci responded. "I'm still waiting for him to make an honest woman of me."

"How long have you been awake, Smarty Pants?" Bill asked.

"Long enough to know you spent all night here."

"Don't believe a word she says," Bill said to the nurse. I've been trying to marry this woman since the day I met her and she won't let me."

"Now who is telling tall tales?"

"You ready to go home, Ms. Sanders?" the doctor asked, as he entered the room.

"Yes, I am."

The doctor handed Traci a prescription and assured her that he was available if she had needed anything.

"Bill?"

"Yes, baby?"

"You think there's a chance we can get Darren to come back for the wedding?"

"Are you kidding? Your brother adores you. You tell him you want him here and he'll be here."

"I hope so."

"All it takes is a phone call."

"I don't know about that these days with Darren. It's impossible to reach him. He has no landline at all and his cellphone number seems to change constantly."

"I guess you'll just have to leave a voicemail message at the last number you have for him. You pile on enough guilt and he'll be here. Once he hears you're in the hospital, he won't be able to help coming home."

"You obviously don't know my brother. That would never work with him."

"In fact, I know exactly how to get Darren here."

While the hospital prepared Traci's discharge papers Bill found the loudest area of the hospital to call Darren. He scrolled through the call log on her cell phone and located the last number she dialed with a Mississippi area code and hit redial.

Bill was quite surprised when a man with a deep Southern accent answered the phone. It was obviously not Darren.

"Uh, I'm not sure if I have the right number. Is Darren Sanders there?"

"Hold on."

"Darren, it's for you."

"Hi, Darren. It's Bill. Traci is in the hospital. She had a miscarriage."

"Is she okay?" Darren asked.

"She's fine, but she was asking for you."

"Really?"

"Yeah. She asked me if I thought you would come back for the wedding."

"If that's what she wants, you can tell her yes, I'll do my very best to get back to New York for her wedding."

"Yes! That is going to mean so much to her. She's sort of in the dumps and could definitely use something to lift her spirits. This will be exactly what she needs. I can't wait to tell her."

Suddenly Darren felt conflicted. When he visited New York, he had established an immediate disliking for his sister's fiancé. However, after listening to him on the phone, so excited about being able to bring good news to Traci, he couldn't help but wonder if he had misjudged him. It was obvious Bill loved his sister very much.

By the time Bill returned to Traci's room she had gotten her discharge papers and was ready to leave.

"Guess what, *soon-to-be* Mrs. Bianco?"

"What?"

"Your brother will be walking you down the aisle."

"How do you know that?"

"I called him. I figured what better time to ask someone a favor than from a hospital bed."

"Are you sure you're not a Jewish mother? You are positively shameless; using illness and guilt to get someone to say yes to something."

"I simply utilized the resources at my disposal. It worked, didn't it?"

When the orderly showed up with the wheelchair, Traci assured him she didn't need one.

"Sorry, but you have to get in," he said. "It's hospital policy."

"Does the hospital mind if I push?" Bill added.

"Absolutely not. Just as long as someone is pushing her in this chair we're good."

"You're enjoying this, aren't you?" Traci asked.

"Enjoying what?"

"You know what; the fact that I'm helpless and defenseless."

"I could never enjoy a thing like that."

Traci took some time off from work and, for the first couple of days, she slept. By the third day she was climbing the walls and was happy when she heard her doorbell ringing. She was happy to have a visitor, but surprised to find it was Bill's mother at the door.

"Haven't the two of you had any luck finding a house?" she asked as soon as she entered the apartment.

"Bill saw a place in Jersey he liked but I would prefer Long Island. I would like being able to teach at a Long Island school at some point."

Candace knew that was only part of the reason she preferred Long Island to New Jersey. The thought of living too close to her was probably more than the girl could stand.

"Really?" was all Candace said.

"You know, Bill won't be home for hours. He's at work."

"Yes, I know. I came to see you. Bill mentioned you might need some company and I was going to stop by anyway. I had an idea I wanted to run by you."

"What's that?"

"Bill mentioned to me that you hadn't found a place to have the wedding and I thought maybe you might want to get married at our house."

Traci had to admit, it would be a beautiful place to have a wedding, but she wasn't anxious for Bill's mother to take over.

Candace knew exactly what her future daughter-in-law was thinking. "You would be free to set up things however you'd like and things would be easier since you'll have the house staff at your disposal. And, you won't have to worry about me butting in, because I'm not the wedding planner type."

"Oh no, I wasn't thinking..."

Candace put up her hand as if to cut her off. "Don't give it a thought. So, how have you been?"

"Okay, I guess."

"You and I have something in common."

"We do?"

"Yes, we do. Bill's father and I couldn't have children. It seemed like every time I got pregnant, something went wrong."

"And, then you had Bill."

"Yes, and then we had Bill," Candace added.

"How did you feel after? I've heard other women talk about having a miscarriage and I never realized how much it hurts. I keep thinking about this little person that I never even got a chance to see and now he or she is gone. It seems so unfair. Many of the parents at the school I teach at are caring and loving parents, but there are some that should have never had children. Yet, they have a pack. I keep asking myself why it had to be my baby that died. It feels like this feeling will never go away."

"It will, dear. You *will* get pregnant again and you *will* have a baby of your own. You have to have faith."

"Wow, that's the same thing my mother said."

"See, dear, I'm not so different than your mother or any other woman you know. People always talk about men and how strong they are, but it's women that carry all the strength. We carry such loads, trying to be everything for everyone; mother, wife, daughter, that some of us turn around and realize that while we were taking care of everyone else, we somehow got lost in the shuffle. I think that's why I've always felt like when all is said and done, sometimes being a bitch is all some women have left."

Traci couldn't believe this was the first real conversation she had ever had with Bill's mother.

"Oh, Mrs. Bianco, forgive my bad manners. Did you want something to drink, maybe a cup of coffee?"

"You're the patient. I'll make the coffee. Have a seat. Will you have a cup with me?"

"I've been drinking chamomile tea. I find it calms me."

"Tea it is."

By the time Bill came home from work he was surprised to find his mother had not only come by to check on Traci, but she was still there.

"What have you ladies been up to all day?" he asked.

"I was just telling Traci about the best school districts in New Jersey."

"Really?"

"Really," Candace responded.

CHAPTER SEVENTEEN

*T*raci and Bill had a very small wedding at his mother's home and Candace kept her word and didn't interfere with any of the planning. Traci was happy that Darren also kept his word and showed up to give her away. He stayed with them a couple of days before the wedding and she hoped that he would stick around a while after the wedding, but he was gone the next day. Within a couple of months of getting married, they found their dream home; a three-bedroom house in Long Beach, Long Island.

From the moment they moved into their home, Traci began grappling with her plans for the future. She loved teaching at the inner-city school she had been at since she started and thought the kids there *really* needed her, but there was a part of her that wanted to try something different. She was thinking more and more about making life easier for herself and that meant not only working closer to home but also working at a school that wasn't quite as *challenging*. While she attempted to make the right decision, her mind was made up for her.

Sandra Piper called a meeting one Thursday morning.

"I'm sure most of you are aware of the fact that our school is one of the schools that has been considered for closing. The Mayor and the Board of Education have gone back and forth over this decision for the past few years and now something has been decided.

We will be closing. Most of you will be relocated to new schools and this location will eventually be revamped into another school. I want to reassure each and every one of you that this is no one's fault. The factors that create a poorly performing school are vast and obviously none of us wanted our school to be on such a list, but it is what it is. In the meantime, there will be a transitional period, of course, and I hope all of you will reach out to me if there is anything at all I can do to make that transition an easier one."

Traci couldn't help but think that this was one of the moments when fate had intervened.

In the months that followed Traci went about the task of looking for a teaching job in Long Island and said her good-byes to the staff and students. In some respects she was thankful that the school had closed. At least that way the kids would not have to deal with the fact that she, like so many other people in their lives, had abandoned them.

Traci watched as Sandra walked toward her and realized how much she would miss seeing her mentor every day.

"This better not be good-bye," Traci said.

"Bitch, I'm coming to your house tomorrow," Sandra joked.

"Shhh. Do you want the kids to hear you?" Traci cautioned.

"Hell, these kids have said and heard ten times worse than that. Besides, this isn't our school any more. The Board of Ed and that asshole Mayor can't tell me what to do."

"What are you going to do? Do you think you'll be able to get something as a principal at another school?"

"I'm going to take a break. I've got some money saved. I think I'll head down South to visit family. You know, fight the good fight. When I come back, I'm going to try the private sector."

"Really? I never figured you for a private sector kind of a girl?"

"As much as I hate to admit it, even I get tired of fighting all the time. Eventually, I'm going to need to take a little break."

"I can understand that."

"When I get back into town, I'll call you," Sandra said.

"Sounds good; Bill and I will fix you a nice traditional Italian dinner."

"Wow, I'm not even going to get into how comical that sentence was."

"Have a good trip! If you should be anywhere near Mississippi, look Darren up. I worry about that boy."

"I'll be sure to do that."

As Sandra reached the exit, she turned and blew Traci a kiss.

"Can you believe it?" Traci shouted. "After almost two and a half years, it ends not with bang but with a whisper."

As the door closed behind Sandra, Traci turned around and took one last look at the school she always saw as dilapidated. For some reason, today, it looked like the most beautiful thing she had ever seen. The tears she never expected to come fell, just in time for Kevin Smith to see her. He raised both his hands and shrugged, as if to say what are you gonna do? Traci hoped he would be okay. She remembered the first time she had spoken to Sandra and something she said about saving them all. Traci knew she couldn't save them all individually, but for now, she would at least keep tabs on this one.

"Hey, Kevin, come here for a second."

Traci had to smile. He was all decked out in designer duds and his usual two-hundred-dollar kicks. In the past two years he had added a manly gait to his ensemble.

"Yeah, Ms. Sanders? What's up?"

"Here, Kevin; take my number. If you should every need *anything* will you promise me you'll call?"

"Okay."

"No, seriously Kevin, I mean it. Promise me, okay?"

"Yeah, yeah, I promise."

Traci stepped closer to hug him and Kevin made a joke about stepping on his shoes.

"Boy, you better come here and give me a hug."

As she walked away, Kevin called to her. "Ms. Sanders?"

"Yes, Kevin?"

"You were the best teacher I ever had."

"And you were my favorite student."

"Hey, I thought you told me once that teachers don't have favorite students."

"I lied."

Kevin laughed.

When Traci got home, Bill was waiting for her with dinner on the table.

"Did you get home early today?" she asked.

"Yeah, I told everyone I had to cook dinner for my wife tonight."

"Is it a special occasion?"

"No, I was missing you all day and I figured you would need a quiet, home-cooked meal after today."

"Can you believe that after all the soul searching I was doing about whether or not I wanted to work here on the Island or in the City, today was so hard?"

"I believe it. You're a good teacher, who cares about her kids. It makes perfect sense."

"I don't know what I'm going to miss more; Sandra and her philosophical discussions, those special kids like Kevin Smith, or that hard ass chair I had to sit on all day. I actually considered taking the fucking chair with me. I'm such a sap."

"No, you're not. You are a sensitive soul with a heart of gold. I knew that from the very first moment I met you."

"Wow! Remember that? If someone had told me then that you and I would be married and living out on Long Island one day, I would have told them they were crazy."

"I wouldn't. I always knew."

"No, you didn't."

"Yes, I did."

"Oh yeah? What about Eleanor?"

"Eleanor was a *checklist item*."

"What the fuck does that mean?" Traci said, laughing.

"Everyone expected it. Eleanor expected it, my mother expected it. Even the people we work with all expected Eleanor and me to get together. So, when you and I split up, it seemed like something I should probably do."

"Uh, huh; and how often did you *do* her?"

"Are you asking me what I think you're asking me? Mrs. Bianco, do you want to know how often Eleanor and I boned?"

"Yeah, how often?"

Bill laughed. "Let me put it to you this way, what Eleanor and I did wasn't as much boning as it was a military exercise. Ten Hut! Pinch my nipples, flick it to the right, flick it to the left. Enter me. Ten hut! Then, go in, then out—three times. Change position. Ten hut!"

"That is so wrong on so many levels."

"It may be wrong but it is true."

Traci leaned in and kissed Bill full on the lips. "You want some military boning tonight, baby?"

"Ten hut!"

After about a year Bill and Traci had settled comfortably into their new home. Traci was teaching at a local school and Bill's business was booming. They had even established a workable routine with Bill's mother. They still visited her for dinner on Sundays, but it had been cut down to one Sunday a month. In turn, Traci and Bill would cook dinner for her at their place at least once or twice a month. Bill was happy with how well his mother and Traci were getting along and, on occasion, the two of them even got together without Bill, to shop or go to brunch.

One day Traci came home from work to find Bill sitting in the office in front of the computer rubbing his head and cursing.

"Baby, what's wrong?"

"These fucking militant groups have been trying to start trouble since that explosion."

"Are you talking about the Empire State Building?"

"Of course."

"I don't get it. Why are you so upset?"

"This one group in particular has been relentless since day one. They've accused my company of everything, including murder."

Traci pulled up a chair and began reading the blog posting Bill was looking at. The group's name jumped out at her immediately. Color of Change was the group Darren was connected to. Whoever had written the blog insinuated that only Bill's company, Satellite Security, could have planted the explosives that brought the Empire State Building down and killed thousands.

"I lost my fucking home in that explosion. Hell, I could have lost my life. That's the problem with technology and blogs like these. People can write whatever they want without fear of retribution. I swear I should sue these motherfuckers."

"Who would you bring a lawsuit against? It's not like organizations like these have a President or a CEO or anything."

"You'd be surprised at what organizations like this have and what they're capable of. Reading this article, they know more about the inner workings of my company than I'm comfortable with. Someone has to be leaking information. It doesn't make any sense."

Traci tried to remember if she had shared any of Bill's business information with Darren. Then she realized she couldn't have. She didn't know anything.

After she and Bill had gone to bed, Traci got up in the middle of the night and called Darren. She dialed the last number she had for him and was happy to find that it was still a working number.

"Darren, it's me."

"Hi, me."

"You're in a good mood and you sound wide awake."

"I could say the same about you and the wide awake part. Not so much the good mood part, though."

"You'd be right about that."

"What's up?"

"Bill is a little upset?"

"Yeah, about what?"

"There's a blog online, written by someone at the COC. It blames Bill's company for the Empire State Building explosion."

"Really?"

"Darren, you said once that you know me well. You know that works both ways and I know you just as well. Did you have anything to do with that blog? I know you at least were aware that it existed even before I called you."

"Yes, you're right. I was aware of it, but I had nothing to do with the content," he lied.

"I'm so glad to hear that. I have to know that I can trust you, Darren. I've never questioned any aspect of our trust for one another before. I would hate to have to begin to question it now."

"You don't."

"Good."

When Traci returned to the bedroom, she was surprised to find Bill watching the news on the television.

"What are you doing up?" she asked. "Couldn't you sleep?"

"I woke up and you weren't there. What are you doing up?"

"You know me. I woke up with my mind spinning; thinking about Darren, thinking about my mother. So, I decided to call Darren and check on him."

"Is everything okay?"

"Yeah, Darren is fine. I'll check on my mother tomorrow."

"That's probably a good idea. That storm that's been predicted seems to be heading straight for us. We should all probably get prepared."

"Really? Do you think it's going to be as bad as they're predicting?"

"It sure sounds that way. It will probably be more of an issue for us than for your mother, but it makes sense to follow all precautions. In the meantime, let's try to get some sleep."

CHAPTER EIGHTEEN

*A*ll weekend the news coverage was all about Hurricane Molly. Despite officials' efforts to get everyone to prepare and in many cases to evacuate, not everyone complied.

Traci's mother reassured her that she would be fine and put her mind at ease by explaining how prepared she was with candles and plenty of food and water.

Traci and Bill were both convinced it was all hype and were reluctant to abandon their home, so they decided to wait it out. When the Mayor made the decision to shut down MTA subways and buses on Sunday afternoon and evening, the potential for a much more serious storm than they both anticipated began to materialize. Yet, they still declined to evacuate their Long Beach home, as suggested. All of the schools, including the New York City Public Schools, were shut down on Monday. Bill did have some work to do, which he did from home while they both kept up with the progress of the storm.

Bill was in and out of his home office, checking on the storm in the living room, where Traci was watching television.

"Bill, sit down and watch this with me. I'm starting to think we should have evacuated."

"There's still time," Bill said.

"Are you sure? I don't know if we should go or stay at this point. Look at this. Bill and Traci watched *ABC News* to get the most up-to-the-minute information."

"As we come on air, you can see it swirling right over my shoulder here, what's being called a super storm tonight. Hurricane Molly is more than two hundred miles off the coast, about to crash into two other systems when it makes landfall. And look at this picture tonight. This is from space, from NASA. It's a massive storm, one thousand miles across. Long before it makes landfall sometime tomorrow night, it is already being felt all along the coastlines. Whipping winds and rains have flooded many communities. The number of Americans impacted by this storm will be enormous. Sixty million people, really anyone east of the Mississippi, will be affected. Hundreds of thousands have already been evacuated tonight. This evening, we've learned schools are already closed for two million children tomorrow across seven states and Washington, D.C., as they all ask now, what about Halloween? Tonight, the potential danger zone, is reaching eight hundred miles inland from the East Coast. This evening, blizzard warnings have gone up in some parts of some states. And the third view, you can see our extreme weather team on all of this tonight. Sam Champion has the track in just a moment here, but let's begin with ABC's Matt Gutman. Matt?"

"Good evening, David. From a very wet, loud and surprisingly cold North Carolina, we've been feeling these fifty-mile-per-hour gusts of wind. Now, Hurricane Molly, this is not a glancing blow, even though it's over two hundred and sixty miles offshore, we've been feeling the rain and wind and you can see the waves exploding onto the pier behind me. Now, a number of communities here in the outer banks have been cut off, like Cape Hatteras because of flooding. Notice the white foam? It kind of looks like snow; this has all been churned up by that rising sea. A lot of people consider tropical systems, they are warm, but this is cold. All this icy air is pushing northward, David."

"All right, taking a beating there in North Carolina, Matt Gutman, our thanks to you tonight. Why is everyone calling this a super storm, and where is the track right now? Let's bring in ABC's Sam Champion. He's in Lower Manhattan tonight, where there could be a huge storm surge. Sam, if you will, let's start with the track. Where is Molly right now?"

"Yes, sir, David. Hey, David, that picture you showed behind you on the cloud canopy. I just have to mention that the clouds stretch from the Carolinas all the way to Hudson Bay and almost to the Arctic Circle. This is an impressive, incredible cloud canopy. One of the largest we've seen in the Atlantic Hurricane Basin. Let me show you the track. We've only seen a little wobble, a little change in the last few forecast paths, and they are still expected to make the turn toward the coastline and find the spot right around Atlantic City, by two o-clock in the morning. That's been the spot that's been going up and down the Jersey Shore a little bit. But right now, that's where it settled. Follow it, running all the way into Maine, just north of Maine, David, by the time we get to Friday."

"All right, the latest track tonight, Sam. So, why is this a super storm? Why is it combining here to create such a massive system?"

"That's a really good question. It is kind of easier to show you, so, here is what we did, David. We took a couple of things, put it into a 3d graphic, and here is what makes this storm a super storm. All night long, Molly marches up the East Coast, practically parallel. More than two hundred miles offshore, it will collide with an arctic front, coming in from the west, throwing a new dose of energy into this storm and expanding its already monster size and reach. Then, inject the one-hundred-and-fifty-mile-an-hour plus winds of the jet stream. Forecasters think Molly then explodes into a super storm. So, it's difficult to categorize this storm other than a super storm. It's a hurricane and then some. But it has all the effects that a hurricane would have. Let's start with surge.

"First, where I'm standing right here could have an eleven, eleven and a half feet of additional water in New York Harbor. We looked it up to see if that had happened before. We only found ten feet in New York Harbor in 1960 as a surge. So, it seems to be unprecedented. Look at the storm surf and its reach, all the way up from Rehoboth Beach well north into the coast of Maine. Then, look at the winds. We think the winds will be hurricane force, as they go from Norfolk to Washington and all the way up to Boston. Sixty- to eighty-mile-an-hour winds go all the way to Pittsburgh. Driving rains will be a problem, lots of it, from Pittsburgh to New York to Washington, D.C. to Norfolk—six to eight inches of rain. Some people will see more than a foot of rain from this storm."

"Sam, just before we came on the air, you told me about blizzard warnings tonight?"

"Yeah, that's unbelievable. The National Weather Service in Charleston, West Virginia, put this out. One to two feet above three thousand feet expected in the mountains of West Virginia, Virginia and Maryland. Six states, Pennsylvania, Virginia, West Virginia, North Carolina, Tennessee, and Kentucky, already have issued winter storm watches or warnings for the snow that will be on the back cold side of this system as it pulls away, David."

"All right, Sam. Look for you later in this broadcast. In the meantime, as you heard Sam report there, Molly will most likely come ashore right near Atlantic City in New Jersey sometime tomorrow night. Major evacuations are underway today."

"ABC meteorologist, Ginger Zee, right there in a very wet Atlantic City tonight. Ginger, good evening."

"David, you can see the boardwalk is lined with sandbags. The casinos, they're empty. We're in the nine- to eleven-foot storm surge zone. We could get ten- to twenty-foot waves. This whole thing could be under water Tuesday morning. We really are at ground zero when that beast comes onshore. It's a mandatory ghost town in Atlantic City—the iconic boardwalk, boarded up, the customary ka-ching of casino floors, silent. Tolls were waved to get people out fast. Buses lined up to take those who couldn't leave on their own to the shelters around the city. They're preparing here for a direct hit. We got to get the boards up because of the weather."

"You don't intend to leave?"

"We couldn't find anywhere to go. We didn't want to be in a shelter. So, the best place is the house right now. We found John and his friend borrowing sand from the beach and bringing it home. Trying to block up the house and not let the water in, you know?"

"So, you figured, just come grab it from the beach?"

"Right, right. We have to use these trash bags for now. Dan lives right on the shore but he's getting out."

"You're worried?"

"Yeah, I'm really worried because they told a friend of mine that they think it's going to hit the bay, the bay and the ocean are going to come together. Much of the more than two hundred miles of the Jersey Shore is a series of sliver-like barrier islands, with water on both sides. So, the concern isn't just about storm surge piling up from the ocean. It's also about storm surge coming off of bays like this one, pushing into homes like these on the other side of these narrow islands. The storm arrives at a bad time, too, when there's a full moon. That means tides will be especially high and any surge will be especially dangerous. Lancaster, Baltimore, those are all areas that will have inland flooding—it won't just be coastal. Remember that, too."

Traci turned down the sound, leaving the television on in case there was a new development.

"You know we can turn this, if you'd like," Bill suggested.

"I think I will. I don't think I can watch any more of this."

Within hours, Traci and Bill had no choice. There was no power and water was reaching their home at an alarming rate.

"What should we do?" Traci asked.

"We need to leave."

"But didn't the Mayor say the time to evacuate had passed?"

"I think potential drowning trumps that idea."

"Where can we go? How?"

"Do you have a phone number for that couple we met that lives in the apartment building nearby?"

"Are you talking about Jim and Trudy?"

"Yeah, Jim and Trudy. Do you have their number?"

"Yeah, I think I do; Judy and I went shopping together a couple of weeks ago."

Traci pulled out her cell phone and nothing. It was the same with Bill's. The phones weren't working.

"What are we going to do?" Traci asked.

"We're going to have to take our chances and hope they're there."

They were in luck. Jim and Trudy Parsons had also not evacuated and Bill and Jim were both relatively confident that the building would be able to withstand whatever was coming. They couldn't have been more wrong. Though the apartment building wasn't as close to the water as Bill and Traci's home, the building began to take in water very quickly and it was a short matter of time before the ground floor was completely flooded. The two couples' only hope was that it would not reach the fourth-floor apartment.

CHAPTER NINETEEN

ill and Traci fared better than most. Although their home was ruined, as new homeowners, they had at least secured full coverage for their home and were well aware of what kind of coverage they possessed. Many of the homeowners in their community had been there so long they couldn't even remember what kind of coverage they had. Even with full coverage, Bill was beginning to wonder if it would make any difference at all, given how things were shaping up. FEMA had come through their community, but it was a long wait before most homeowners saw any really tangible assistance.

Financial loss due to the storm was upwards of $8 billion and at least two hundred people were killed in New York alone.

It had been more than a year since Molly hit and New York was still rebuilding, not to mention other states. The blow to the overall economy was crippling.

It took time, but like so many others, eventually Bill and Traci's life on Long Island seemed to be returning to normal.

"What are you doing home?" Bill asked.

"There were budget cuts and I was the first to go. Can you believe that? Once again I'm out of a job."

"Don't worry, you'll find another job."

"You're much more confident than I am. It's rough out there, baby. The unemployment rate is out of control."

"I have confidence in you. *You* will find something. And, if you want to take a break until things get better, that's an option."

"Are you sure, Bill? You mentioned the other day that you lost two clients. Won't that affect us as well?"

"We're good."

Whenever Traci asked Bill about money, he always said they were good. When she met him he lived modestly, but it seemed over time he was living a lot less so. She wondered if his security firm could be doing that well. Even the largest and most successful companies were in trouble. Every day thousands were being downsized and there seemed to be no relief in sight.

"You know, now might be a good time to think about trying again."

"Yeah, I thought about that too."

"Really!" Bill said excitedly.

"Really."

"So, let's get to it!"

"Bill Bianco, you are insatiable."

"I'm a little scared."

"Aw honey, it's going to be fine. I told you we're going to be fine."

"I'm afraid of getting pregnant again. What if it happens again? What if I have another miscarriage?"

"You heard what the doctor and your mother said. These things are just flukes. Chances are you'll get pregnant and we'll have a beautiful, healthy little quarterback."

"Or a beautiful, healthy little princess."

"Really? Are there really open positions for princesses?"

"Yes, there are."

"Whatever you say, Mama."

"I like the sound of that."

"Well, then, you know what they say, *there's nothing to it but to do it.*"

"Are you sure you're ready for this? The first time was unplanned. Now, we have the luxury of planning. It seems all I've read about recently is the downturn in the economy. Are you sure this is the best time to take on what will shape up to be a huge financial responsibility?"

"What do I have to do to reassure you that we are okay? My father left a great deal of money in trust for me. It's more than enough for the two of us, and anyone else that comes along, to live *very* comfortably for years to come. Even if Satellite Security goes belly up tomorrow, which I don't think is going to happen, we'll still be okay. We're better than okay."

"Why haven't you ever told me this?"

"I don't know. I guess in some respects I'm a little ambivalent about the money. Quite frankly, I was surprised when I found out he had left me anything."

"Why would you be surprised? He was your father."

"My father hated me. He hated me and he hated my mother. I don't know why, but he did."

"Oh, Bill, I find that hard to believe. Not all parents are the best at showing love and affection, but I've never seen a parent that truly hated their own child. Even the very worst parents don't hate their children."

"Yet, there is always an exception to every rule. In this case, I think my father was the exception."

Traci looked at Bill with new eyes. Suddenly, so many things became much clearer. It explained so much about his relationship with his mother. It made sense that he would be bound to her in the way that he was. If he grew up feeling this way his entire life, his mother would have been what he clung to.

Traci reached over and embraced him. Bill's body went limp. It was as if he were a child all over again.

"You are going to be a wonderful father."

"I hope you're right. Let's hope history doesn't repeat itself."

"We won't even talk about that because I know there isn't even a slight chance that will happen. I don't think I've ever known anyone more loving and caring than you. You are going to be an incredible father. I say we get started now. How about you?"

Bill turned down the lights and walked over to the fireplace and lit a fire.

They sat together on the floor, in front of the couch, holding hands and gazing at the flickering flames from the fire.

"I love you, Bill Bianco."

"I love you, Traci Bianco."

Traci wasn't sure if it was the heat emitting from the flames or the desire that radiated between them, but the warmth of Bill's lips was like nothing she ever felt.

"You're so beautiful," Bill whispered. He gazed at her with such love and passion in his eyes, Traci shivered in anticipation. "We'll remember tonight for the rest of our lives."

He slid slowly inside of her. His motions were slow and deliberate as he exalted in the heat enveloping his rigid member. "Baby, you're so hot around me. You're on fire."

Bill rose up, gazing in Traci's eyes as he took up a rhythm, sliding in and out of her. One look into his eyes and Traci tightened around him. A flood of her juices gushed forward, soaking him. Her body gave in to the immense pleasure she was feeling and she convulsed under him. Bill kissed her lips, his tongue taking up the same beat of his member and he exploded inside of her. He barely had enough energy to move and for a moment thought even his voice would need time before he could speak. But he did.

"We just made a baby."

It didn't take long for Traci and Bill to find out he was right. After two home pregnancy tests and a visit to her gynecologist, it was confirmed that Traci was indeed pregnant. Traci was happy she hadn't decided to look for another job. She was going to be a mother.

Because of her earlier miscarriage, Traci wanted to wait until at least her second trimester before she told anyone.

"Bill, honey, could you pick my mom up from the station? She's coming in on the railroad."

"Yeah, of course. What time?"

"I think her train gets in at one fifty-five."

"What are you girls up to today?"

"I think we're going to hit the mall, but I was going to fix lunch here first and this place needs cleaning, desperately. I feel like I'm turning into a little piglet."

"You're tired. It's understandable. It's the pregnancy."

"Now that's one more thing I love about you. There you go making excuses for my shoddy housekeeping."

"The house is fine. Every now and then you just have to say fuck it. Besides, I'd rather you rest. In fact, I was going to suggest we hire someone. You're going to need help anyway once the baby gets here."

"I'll be fine. We don't need a housekeeper."

"Baby, you've earned the right to take it easy. Let me take care of you."

"Okay."

By the time Bill got back from the station with Traci's mother, she had tidied up the house a bit and made salmon burgers and a salad for lunch.

"Hi, Mama!"

"Hi, baby! How does it feel to be a woman of leisure?"

"I'm getting used to it."

"Good for you."

"Bill, honey, are you going to have lunch before you go?"

"No thank you, babe. I'll get something outside. Have fun shopping."

"We will. I'll see you later."

Traci prepared the table for lunch and her and her mother sat down to eat. Traci had three salmon burgers, a salad and a slice of cheesecake for dessert.

"So when's the baby due?" her mother asked.

Traci almost spit out the cheesecake she was eating. "Huh?"

"Don't huh me. I've got eyes. Don't you ever forget; Mama sees all."

"I'm three months."

"Well, congratulations. See, I told you; your time will come. Pretty soon you'll be a mother and I'll be a grandmother!"

Traci glanced at the newspaper in her mother's bag.

"Mom, can I see that?"

"Of course."

The headline read: *Economic Devastation Ahead: Stock Market Crashes.*

CHAPTER TWENTY

With all of Bill's talk of not being worried about money, Traci knew he was in fact very worried. She heard the phone conversations he had with his colleagues and his mother when he thought Traci was out of earshot.

"We should sell now!"

Traci wasn't sure who was on the other end of the line, but whoever it was obviously didn't agree with Bill.

"If we sell now, we can all get out before we have nothing. My father built this company from nothing. I'd rather sell it at a loss now than wait too long and have nothing. If we wait any longer, that's what will happen. Mom, just do me a favor and look everything over and think about it. But, don't think too long. We don't have much time."

Traci walked away before Bill became aware that she was listening. She waddled over to the couch and lay down.

"Can I get you anything, baby? Maybe another pillow?"

"No, I'm okay. I just wish this kid would come already. She's a stubborn little thing, like her daddy."

"You mean just like her mother. Speaking of stubborn, did you get a chance to speak to your mother again about coming to stay here?"

"I did. She won't listen. I don't know what else to do. Things have gotten worse over there. She's still working at the housing project and not getting paid. I've tried speaking to everyone I can think of; anyone that can tell me that what is happening is a breach of some kind of law or something. Undoubtedly, it is not and my mother is suffering each day. She's too old to be doing that kind of work. She's diabetic and she's been slipping with taking her insulin. The last time I was over there, she went in the bathroom and tried to hide it from me, but when I walked in, she was taking off her socks and shoes and her feet were a mess. I'm so afraid she's going to mess around and lose a toe or something; or even worse than that, her whole leg."

"Traci, at this point, maybe you have to insist. I mean, if you have to claim illness yourself to get her to stay here, then maybe that's what you have to do."

"You don't know, Bill. I've tried everything. She's scared of something. I really do think someone is strong-arming not only my mom but the other tenants as well. What I don't understand is why no one has done anything."

"People are scared. It's bad out there. Even my mother had to let some of her staff go. Two members of her staff were so desperate, they asked if they could come back and have been working for food and shelter. From what I've been hearing her situation is not an isolated one. There are plenty of people that are doing the same."

"Oh my God! How could I be so blind?"

"It's not just you. The media has been getting pressure from government officials to keep a lid on how bad things are. I've never seen anything like it. In fact, I've been considering selling the company. My mother is digging her heels in, but we're going to have to. The fucked up thing is, at this point, I don't even know if we'll be able to. And, if we do we're surely going to take a huge loss."

"What does this mean to us; to the baby?"

"Our stocks have taken a hit like everyone else's, but I still think with whatever we can make from the sale of Satellite and what we have in savings and my trust fund, we'll be fine."

"Why didn't you tell me things had gotten that bad?"

"Traci, you're pregnant. I didn't want you to worry. I want you to concentrate on having a healthy baby; that's all. I can take care of us. Just leave it all to me. Now, let me get us something to eat. Isn't little Caitlin or Veronica hungry yet?"

"Starving."

Traci lay on the couch while Bill busied himself in the kitchen. She was afraid for their future for the first time in a long time. She was not only afraid for her, Bill and the baby, but for the entire world and especially for people like her mother.

Traci was two weeks overdue for her delivery and she was starting to get antsy. All of the news on the television was bad and she found herself slipping into a bit of a depression, when as if in answer to her prayers, she got a call from Sandra.

"Oh my God, Sandra! Where are you? It's been ages."

"I'm back in New York. How are you doing?"

"I'm okay. Waiting for this baby to pop."

"I can't wait to see you. You up for some company?"

"Up for some company? I've been going stir crazy. This little lady is two weeks overdue."

"Aw. You're having a girl."

"Yeah, and obviously a stubborn little girl."

"You're going to be a good mama."

"I hope you're right. It's the damndest thing. I've had nine plus months to prepare and now I'm getting scared."

"That's completely normal."

"That's what everyone keeps telling me. Say, is there a chance I could put you to work?"

"Anything."

"Bill is out for a few but he's supposed to come back and take me to the doctor. I would much rather you take me. I have just enough time to call him and stop him from coming home."

"What's going on? Is everything okay between you two?" Sandra asked.

"We're fine, but I don't know if it was the miscarriage I had or just the normal worries of a prospective father, but he's getting on my last nerve. He watches me like I'm a boiling pot of water. It's unnerving."

"I would love to go with you. It'll give me a chance to live precariously through you. I'm so jealous."

"No need to be jealous, god mommy."

"Really?"

"Really, if you want to."

"Hell yeah, I want to. I'm going to spoil that little princess rotten."

"Do you have a car?" Traci asked.

"Yes. I just need directions."

After hanging up with Sandra, Traci called Bill. "Hey, babe."

"Oh, hey, Kitten."

"You okay?" she asked.

"Yeah, I'm fine."

"You sound a little distracted."

"Just work stuff; nothing for you to worry about. What's up?"

"I'm calling about the doctor's appointment."

"Oh shit! I forgot about that."

"No worries. I was calling to tell you that Sandra's going to take me."

"Sandra?"

"Yeah, don't tell me you forgot Sandra, the principal at my first school?"

"Oh, yeah, yeah. Now I remember."

"I can't believe you forgot her that quick. She's the one who got me to the hospital when I lost the baby."

"Don't talk about that," Bill said. "It's a bad omen."

"In all the years that we've been together, I don't think I've ever heard you mention anything about omens. Are you sure you're okay?"

"I'm fine, Traci. I'm just fine."

"That's three fines in one conversation; I can see you're busy so I'll let you get back to things."

Traci hung up the phone, worried about what was going on with Bill. He was so secretive and kept so much to himself. With Bill it could be anything from having to terminate an employee to bankruptcy. She'd never know, because he told her nothing about his business dealings. It was like their home was a cocoon that the two of them were secured in and none of his life outside that cocoon ever entered.

Traci tried to tidy up a bit, despite her labored movements. By the time she had done all she was going to do and sat down, Sandra was ringing the doorbell.

"You look beautiful," Sandra said, hugging Traci.

"You don't look so bad yourself. That little vacation you took must have done you some good. You look very rested."

"Damn, girl, you say that like I looked tore up before."

"No! I just mean you look especially rested."

"The funny thing is, I'm not really. I've been working more in the last year than I ever worked as a teacher or a principal."

"You're not working in a school?"

"No. That's one of the reasons I wanted to see you, but we can talk about all of that later. What time is your doctor's appointment?"

"In about a half-hour. It's not far from here."

While Sandra sat in the waiting room, she wondered if she should have held off on mentioning to Traci she had something she wanted to talk to her about. The last thing she wanted to do was upset her in her condition. Just as she began to formulate an alternate story to the one she actually came there to discuss with Traci, a nurse in the doctor's office appeared in the doorway.

"Is there a Sandra Piper here?" she asked.

"Yes, that's me."

"Could you come with me?"

Sandra hoped Traci was okay and realized she was when she walked in the room. Traci was grinning from ear to ear.

"Finally this kid is ready to come out!"

"We're going to transport Mrs. Bianco to the hospital. Would you like to go along with her?"

"Yes. I sure would."

Traci was already on the phone with Bill and he was going to meet her and Sandra at the hospital.

"Hallelujah!" Traci said. "I thought I was going to have to resort to sex to get this watermelon out of me."

"Girl, you are so crazy!"

After all the books Traci had read, as a new mother, she was prepared for her labor to be quite long. Everyone, including her mother, was surprised that after only two and a half hours of labor, little Caitlin Marie Bianco was born. She was nine pounds, eight ounces, twenty-two inches long, a head full of thick black hair and the greenest eyes Traci had ever seen.

Traci's mother didn't make it in time for the delivery, but arrived shortly thereafter. She walked in limping slightly and despite the star of the hour, Caitlin, no one could help but notice that Bertha Sanders did not look well.

"Bertha, come on over here and sit down next to your grand-daughter." Bill got up and gave Bertha his chair, not only because he was a gentleman, but mostly because he didn't think she would be able to stand for longer than a minute or two.

"Thank you, Bill. I practically ran all the way here. I was trying to make it for the delivery. I must look a mess."

Traci knew that her mother's comment was to divert everyone's attention away from what was really going on. "Mama, you look tired," Traci said.

"Now don't you go start worrying about me. You've got plenty to worry about now. You're a mother."

Bertha reached down and stroked her granddaughter's head. "I knew that girl was gonna have *good hair*," she said.

"Oh, Mama, nobody calls it good hair anymore."

"You know what I mean."

A recording announced the end of visiting hours and Sandra, Bill and her mother all kissed her and the baby good-bye.

They had gotten off the elevator and were leaving the building when Bertha collapsed. Bill and Sandra tried to wake her, but she wouldn't respond.

CHAPTER TWENTY-ONE

"Somebody help us," Sandra yelled. She ran into the hospital, trying to get anyone to come and help Traci's mother. No one seemed to be moving quickly enough. "My friend's mother is outside! I think she's dying!"

An attendant grabbed a stretcher and sped outside the door, with an EMT and nurse directly behind him. When he got there, Bill was performing CPR, but judging from the look on his face, it wasn't doing much good.

The EMT took over for Bill and he and Sandra stood watching, their faces filled with fear.

"I'm sorry," the EMT announced. "She's dead."

"Oh my God! Traci!" Sandra said. "What are we going to tell Traci?"

"I don't know. I really don't know. Where are you staying, Sandra?" Bill asked.

"I'm in Brooklyn."

"Do you want to stay at the house? You must be exhausted."

"I don't want to put you out."

"You won't be putting me out at all. In fact, you'll be doing me a favor. I really don't want to be alone tonight and Traci's going to need both of us. This is going to be so hard for her."

"And it will never get easier. My brother died on Christmas Eve. It's been fifteen years and I still get depressed around holiday time. For the rest of her life, her daughter's birthday will be the same day her mother died."

Bill hadn't thought of it that way and now he was even more concerned about Traci. "Please say you'll stay."

"Of course I will. Where else would I be?"

The next morning, the phone rang bright and early. It was Traci.

"Can you believe it? They're pushing me and Caitlin out of here already. They said I could go home today."

It was the first time Bill ever dreaded the prospect of seeing Traci. It didn't occur to him that she would be going home so soon and after he and Sandra got in, it was clear neither of them wanted to talk or even think. Bill got Sandra settled in the guest room and after an hour or so of tossing and turning, he finally drifted off to sleep. It had only been a few hours and he was now forced to explain to his wife, who had just given birth, that her mother was gone.

While Bill was on the phone with Traci, Sandra came in and asked him if he wanted breakfast.

"Is that Sandra? What kind of monkey business have you two been up to?" she joked.

Bill was so deep in thought about what to say to his wife, and when, that he hadn't even heard what Traci said.

"Bill, you still there?"

"Yeah, yes, I'm here."

"Should I be worried? I asked what kind of monkey business you two were up to and not even a chuckle. I hope you've been behaving yourself."

Bill managed a forced laugh.

Traci knew she had no need to be concerned about anything happening between Sandra and Bill, but she sensed that there was something wrong.

"Thanks for making my friend comfortable. I appreciate it. I thought about her driving back from here last night and I hoped you would ask her to stay. I don't know why it didn't occur to me to ask you to do that."

"You had much more important things on your plate. Speaking of which, how's our girl?"

"She's good. The lactation specialist was just here, helping me to breastfeed. I tried last night and Caitlin didn't seem to want my milk."

"Is she okay?"

"Yeah, she's fine. I'm probably just not producing enough milk yet. One of the aides here said I could probably supplement with formula in the meantime; but I don't want to do that. Natural is best."

"I'll defer to you and the medical professionals on such points."

Traci laughed. "Is Sandra standing nearby?"

"Yeah, she's right here."

"Can I speak to her? Oh, also Bill, is my mother there or did you take her home last night?"

Bill panicked when Traci asked about her mother, and handed the phone off to Sandra, hoping she would think he hadn't heard her.

"Hey girl," Traci said. "Is my baby okay? I mean my big baby?"

"He's fine. I'm going to fix us some breakfast now."

"Aw. Thank you, Sandra. Any chance you could stick around a bit longer? I'm getting out the hospital today and we never got a chance to talk. Wasn't there something you wanted to talk to me about?"

"It wasn't anything important," Sandra lied.

"You sure."

"I'm sure. And, of course I'll stick around. I'm in no hurry to go home."

In fact, Sandra wished she could stay even longer, but that was a bad idea. Although she had no intention of putting Traci or her family in danger when she arrived, she did want to discuss with her what had been going on for the past year or so. If Traci wasn't already aware, Sandra knew it was her duty to make her aware. But, given the turn of events over the past couple of days, that would have to wait.

"Good. I'll need all the help I can get. And, it'll be nice to have a conversation about something other than baby stuff. I'm sure my mother will be staying as well, and she can sometimes be a bit much to take. Did you catch her good hair comment in the hospital? I thought I was going to die when she said that. It'll be nice to have you there for a buffer. Speaking of which, is my mother there? I know Bill didn't drive her all the way back into the city last night. She must have stayed the night."

CHAPTER TWENTY-TWO

eyond being inconsolable, Traci was angry. She was angry with Sandra and Bill. She also showed no interest in caring for the baby. She abandoned her desire to breastfeed and instead opted for formula. When Bill commented, she simply snapped at him.

"I bought you a breast pump."

"What on earth for? I told you I'm not breastfeeding. What's the point? My milk was already problematic. Do you think it's now going to get better with all the stress I'm under? She'll be fine. It's not like I'm putting vodka in her bottle. It's formula. Millions of babies drink the same thing."

"It's just I know that's not what you wanted when Caitlin was born."

"I guess things change, don't they? Besides, I've got more important things to do than sit and wait until she's ready to suck on my tit. I've got to bury my mother."

"Traci, Sandra and I both offered to handle all of that for you. You don't have to do this all by yourself."

"Yes, I do. You both treated me like I was some idiot child. I can't trust you to tell me the truth. Why on earth would I let you handle my mother's burial? I can't believe you let my mother sit in that fucking morgue without me knowing a thing. How could you?"

"Traci, if you're going to be mad at anyone, please, be mad at me. I'm your husband. I should have told you. It was a coward's move. I didn't know how to handle it under the circumstances. She collapsed right after you gave birth to Caitlin. I didn't know what it would do to you if I told you that night."

"So, what about the next day? I talked to you on the phone. Here I was all bright and cheery, while my mother was lying dead somewhere. You let me make a fool of myself and you said nothing. Neither of you said a thing."

"Traci, I don't think you should go to your mother's house alone."

"There you go again, managing me. I'm sick of it. I'm sick to death of being managed by you. I'm not a kid. I know nothing about our finances, nothing about anything that doesn't involve these four walls. I guess it's my own fault. I've been working since I was fourteen years old and it was nice not to have to worry about money and worry about a roof over my head, but care is like everything else, even that should be done in moderation. You treat me more like your child than your wife."

"Traci, where is all this coming from? This isn't just about your mother, is it?"

"Damn right it's not! When you told me my mother had died, I realized I had to ask you about insurance, about money, about all the things that I handled myself before we got married. Once upon a time I was a capable and responsible woman. Now, I've been reduced to the *little woman*. It's pathetic."

"And, you blame me for that?"

"A little. I admit I'm responsible for me and it's not all your fault. But, you were just as much a part of this, as I was. Somewhere along the way, I stopped being an equal partner."

"Baby, I can assure you that was never my intention. All I've ever wanted was for us to be equals. And, if I have to spend the rest of our lives proving that to you, I will."

As far as Traci was concerned there was nothing else to say. The ball was in his court.

"I'm going to look for a dress for my mother. I'll see you later. Can you handle Caitlin while I'm gone?"

"Sure."

"I made the bottles already. All you have to do is heat them up. Make sure you test it on your arm first. It should be at room temperature."

"No problem."

As Traci was leaving, Sandra showed up.

"Hi, Traci. You still mad at me?"

It was the meekest she had ever seen Sandra. She couldn't help but drop her angry feelings.

"Don't you ever lie to me again," Traci said.

"Never."

"Can you do me another favor?" Traci asked.

"Sure, anything."

"I have to go to my mother's place. I need to get a dress for her. I'd rather not go alone and I didn't want Bill to go with me. I just started speaking to him again and even if we were speaking, the neighborhood is so weird these days I didn't want to show up at her place with Bill in tow. You understand, don't you?"

"Better than *you know*. Speaking of which, please remind me at some point that I need to speak with you about something. I don't want to do it now. Let's get everything done for your mother first and then we can talk."

"You sure you don't want to do it now?" Traci asked.

"Yeah, I'm sure. It's one of those things that needs a sit down and time. It involves the time I spent down South."

"That's right, we never did get a chance to talk about what you've been doing."

"We will."

Traci and Sandra both noticed that somewhere around Eighty-Sixth Street, all the way up to her mother's place, the police presence seemed to be overkill. On every corner there were at least two uniformed officers.

The sight of men, women and children digging through the garbage searching for food was difficult to see. Traci wanted to take them all home to her place and feed them. One child in particular looked to be no more than four or five years old. He was eating old pizza out of a box. When they arrived at her mother's building, there were not only two officers on every corner, but in front of each building was two more officers, checking identification before anyone was allowed to enter.

"Traci, why don't I wait here until you come back, so we don't have to find parking?"

Traci thought that was a bit strange since when they left, Sandra seemed more than willing to help Traci with something they both knew would be very difficult.

"What's wrong? I thought you were going to come in and help me pick out a dress for my mother."

"It's probably best this way. You'll be able to spend some time alone in your mother's place. You don't need me hanging around."

"I thought that was the whole point, you coming along, so I wouldn't have to be alone?"

"I've had time to think about it and I think it's best this way."

Traci didn't push the issue and got out of the car, her identification in hand.

"I'll try to be quick," she said.

The officer looked Traci over from head to toe.

"Do you live in this building or are you visiting someone?"

"My mother lives in this building; lived in this building. She passed away. I'm coming here to pick up something for her to wear; for the funeral."

"Do you have written permission?" the officer asked.

"Written permission?"

"Yes, it's a building requirement."

"But I have the keys."

The officer was reaching the end of his day and he was anxious to go back to the station and head home. He looked Traci over once again and figured it would be easier and quicker to just let her in than to follow protocol.

"Go ahead up. But, be quick."

Traci didn't know what the hell was going on, but she didn't like it. What right did anyone have to tell her she couldn't go into her own mother's apartment and how long she could stay? She looked around and realized that it was not the time nor the place to question what was taking place.

"I'll be quick."

Once inside the building, Traci was shocked. A list of rules was posted throughout the building. A schedule of work orders for the tenants was also posted along with their names. She noticed that her mother's name, along with several others had been scratched out. She was well aware of why her mother's name had been scratched out but she wondered about the others. She rode the elevator up along with a young man around twelve or thirteen years old. He pressed the twelfth floor.

"What's going on?" Traci asked.

"Huh?"

"What's with all the police and security?"

"Where you been, lady? This is the new world order. Black folks are right back where they started."

The young man got off the elevator and kept on going. Traci

was struck by the fact that all of this seemed to be commonplace for him. She wondered how she could have missed what was happening. She was willing to admit that she hadn't been keeping up with current events as much as she would have liked, but she had been reading newspapers and none of this was mentioned in any of them. For years people that lived in the projects talked about how no one cared about what went on in their corner of the world, but this went way beyond apartments without heat and hot water or drug slayings. What was happening was unlike anything she had ever seen before. Yet, no newspaper she had read recently mentioned any of it.

Traci used her key to open the door to her mother's apartment. It was clear that her mother's place had been ransacked. So many of her things appeared to be missing and the lockbox where her mother kept all of her important papers was gone. In fact, there seemed to be no paperwork of any kind in the apartment at all. It was clear someone was trying to hide something. Traci remembered what the officer had said about being quick and because she had no interest in dealing with the police she went straight to her mother's closet and retrieved an armful of dresses. She didn't even take the time to look through them. She simply closed the door behind her before taking one last look at the home her mother had lived in for so many years.

She was happy to see that the officer she had spoken to coming in was still posted at the door. On her way down on the elevator she wondered if she would have to explain the clothes she was holding in her arms. The officer remembered why she had gone upstairs, looked her over once again and said nothing.

The minute she exited the building, Traci realized the car and Sandra were gone. She juggled the armful of clothes she was holding and retrieved her cell phone from her pocketbook.

"Sandra, where are you?"

"I'm driving around. I'll be right there."

"What happened? Did they ask you to move?"

"No. I didn't give them a chance to. I see you. Stay right there. I'm pulling up now."

Traci opened the back door and tossed the clothes in the seat. She was barely in the car and waiting for Sandra to get out, so she could move over to the driver's seat, when Sandra sped off.

"What's the rush?" Traci asked.

"No rush."

"No rush? You practically left skid marks. Sandra, what the hell is going on?"

"Not now. Let's wait until we get back to your place. Okay?"

"Okay. But, as soon as we get home, I want to know exactly what is going on."

"I promise you, you will."

The moment they entered the house, they were met with Caitlin's cries. Bill was holding her and rocking her back and forth with a bottle in his hand.

"Boy, am I glad to see you," he said. "She won't take the bottle."

"I'll take her."

Traci put the bottle to Caitlin's lips and it only seemed to make her cry more. "I guess she'll eat when she's hungry."

Both Sandra and Bill were surprised at Traci's comment. Most new mothers were usually so worried about caring for a newborn they jumped at every cry. Instead, Traci put Caitlin in her crib, turned on the baby monitor and left.

"Maybe we should take her to the doctor?" Bill asked.

"Did she take any of the bottle today?"

"Very little."

"Little is better than nothing at all. She's fine."

"Traci, are you sure?" Sandra added.

"Yes, I'm sure."

Bill and Sandra exchanged glances while Traci flipped through the dresses she had retrieved from her mother's apartment.

"What do you think of this one, Sandra?" Traci said, holding up a navy blue frock.

"That one is fine."

"Yeah, but does it look like Mama?"

"It looks just like her, honey."

"Then, blue it is."

Traci went back upstairs and Sandra and Bill both assumed she was going to attend to the baby. Instead, they found her going through her own closet.

"What's up?" Sandra asked.

"I'm looking for something to wear to the funeral. This black suit should do it."

"Yeah, that's appropriate."

"You know, I've never understood words like appropriate and suitable when it comes to funerals. How is anything appropriate or suitable when saying good-bye to someone you love?"

"I hear you. Death is one of those inevitable occurrences that none of us will ever get used to."

"I was sitting with the pastor and he was talking about the service and rejoicing and all I kept thinking was, I don't want to fucking rejoice. My mother is dead."

"You know how religious folks are. It's all about meeting their maker."

"Yeah, I guess you're right."

"Traci, I'm not especially religious, but I was thinking about something recently that I guess might be construed as somewhat religious. It's been difficult for you being able to enjoy being a new mother right on the heels of your own mother dying, but I was sitting and thinking about you, Caitlin, and your mother and it occurred to me; three generations of women and even though it's got to hurt to know that your mother died on the very same day your daughter was born, there's something almost celestial about it."

"What are you saying?"

"You know, one soul replacing another—the idea of both your mother and your daughter coexisting in one entity. That thought helps me. I believe it's what's going to get me through tomorrow."

Sandra quickly realized that somehow she had gotten through to Traci. It was something in the expression on her face that said she was ready to let go of the anger and some of the despair and be the kind of mother she always wanted to be.

Sandra assumed she had said enough and got up to leave. "You hungry?" she asked Traci.

"Yeah, I guess I could eat something."

"I'll make you a sandwich."

By the time Sandra returned, Traci was sitting in the baby's room, breastfeeding Caitlin. She was singing a song Sandra was sure she heard before, but couldn't quite place. It started with "Mommies and Daddies always believe..."

CHAPTER TWENTY-THREE

Traci disliked Preston Chambers immediately. There was something swarmy about him. She couldn't help thinking, what rotten taste her brother had in men.

"You did a great job, sis. Thanks for doing all of this," Darren said.

"Well, I couldn't get in touch with you, so I had to."

"Between Sandra and Bill, I got it done. How did you find out anyway; in enough time to make it to the funeral?"

"Bryan got a message to me."

"Got a message to you? What does that mean?"

"It means, I've sort of been living underground. There's a lot of shit going on out there that you know nothing about. I wish I could say that you'll never have to find out personally, but I'm afraid everything that's happening down South is not going to stop there. As we speak, policy makers are taking steps to ensure that our civil rights continue to be violated worldwide."

There was a time when Traci would have chalked Darren's comments up to more of his wild ravings, but she had seen the way things were in her mother's neighborhood. There was definitely something brewing.

Sitting quietly at the viewing, as visitor upon visitor filed in, Traci couldn't help but realize how loved her mother was. It was a packed house. There wasn't a seat to be had, except those for the family, and people were still coming in. Arrangements eventually had to be made for everyone to take seats in the lobby and when those seats were filled, others simply stood.

As Bill, Traci, Darren, and to Traci's dismay, Preston, greeted people as they came in, Traci was overjoyed to see her brother, Sebastian, and her sister-in-law, Angelika arrive.

Traci didn't have much of an opportunity to see Sebastian and Angelika. It was only on the rare occasions when Sebastian was in the States for business that she got to see him. She held on to him for dear life.

"Sebastian! I didn't think you'd be able to make it!"

"Of course I made it. I'm sorry I haven't been more of a presence. I feel like I neglected our mother."

"Stop it, Sebastian. You live all the way in Germany. She knew that you loved her. She did."

"Hi, Angelika."

Angelika and Traci hugged.

"It's been forever," Angelika said. "Where is that beautiful baby? Sebastian and I got the pictures Bill sent to our email."

"My girlfriend, Sandra, has her." Traci scanned the room, looking for Sandra. "There she is."

She pointed to the front row. Traci had asked that Sandra sit with the family, since she considered her as much a member of her family as everyone else. After all, she had been there for just about everything, good and bad, that had happened in her life.

Traci was happy she had snapped out of the fog she had been in. She had exhibited none of the classic traits of a new mother. It hadn't even occurred to her to take pictures of Caitlin. She was happy Bill had thought of it and reached for his hand and squeezed.

Bill looked up, happy that somehow, the old Traci seemed to be resurfacing. He smiled.

"You remember Bill, don't you?"

"We only met the one time, but yes, I do remember Bill," said Angelika.

She kissed Bill on both cheeks.

"Hello, Angelika."

"Hello," Sebastian said, extending his hand. "Nice to see you again, Bill."

"Same here," Bill responded.

"Hey, bro," Darren chimed in.

"Oh my goodness! Look who's resurfaced!"

Sebastian grabbed his brother with such force it almost knocked him off his feet. He had never seen his brother so happy to see him.

"Sebastian, this is Preston, Preston Chambers."

"Very nice to meet you, Preston."

Darren wondered if it was the death of their mother that had softened his brother. It wasn't so long ago that Sebastian demonstrated open distaste for the men in Darren's life.

After all introductions had been made, it was time for the service to start. Bill sat very close to Traci, holding her hand very tightly. At one point, when the Pastor began talking about the family and the birth of Caitlin, in particular, Traci began to cry. She looked down the line of seats for Sandra and before she could say a word, she knew exactly what Traci wanted. She brought Caitlin to her and Traci held onto her baby as tightly as Bill was holding her hand. When the Pastor mentioned the inevitable cycle of life, Traci remembered the words of wisdom Sandra had offered her.

"Bertha Whitman Sanders has moved on to be with our Heavenly Father, but she left a part of her here that will live on in this earthly plane through the love she left behind. Bertha Sanders was loved. That fact is evident as I look around this packed house and the faces of her children and her granddaughter, who was born just hours before Bertha Sanders was called to glory…"

It had always been Traci's belief that the hardest part of any funeral was when the body was lowered into the ground. She learned otherwise when her mother's body was carried out in the casket and placed in the hearse. She tried to hold it together, but one look at her brothers, who were usually so strong, crying; not to mention Bill, and even his mother, was more than Traci could stand. She realized it was a mistake not having anything to eat that morning, when she felt like she might actually pass out. That was the last thing she wanted. This was about her mother and the last thing she wanted or needed was for the focus to be placed on her. She steadied herself against Bill and was able to keep herself from going down.

Sandra must have noticed something because she leaned over and whispered in Traci's ear. "Traci, I have some crackers in my bag if you're feeling a little woozy."

"Thanks, Sandra. I think that would be a good idea. I don't know what I was thinking, not eating this morning."

"You had a lot going on."

"Everything okay?" Bill asked.

"It's okay now," Traci said.

He noticed her nibbling on the crackers and remembered she hadn't eaten before they left the house.

By the time they were in the cars on their way to the burial ground, Traci had gotten it together.

Once at the burial site, Traci couldn't help but see a man staring in their direction. It was the same man she had seen at the funeral. He had been staring at them there also and Traci didn't recognize him at all. She thought she knew all of her mother's friends and this man was not someone she recognized as one of them. He was a white man and seemed to be around thirty or forty years old and was wearing a black wool fedora and a black trench coat.

Traci couldn't swear to it, but she thought she remembered seeing him near her mother's place the day her and Sandra had gone to pick up a dress for her mother to wear. Traci was about to get Sandra's attention, when she turned around and not only was the strange-looking man gone, but so was Sandra, Darren, and even Preston.

The burial complete, everyone returned to Bill and Traci's home.

There was plenty of food and those not too concerned with traveling from the city to Long Island, stopped by to pay their condolences. Some even brought food.

Traci fed Caitlin and laid her down to sleep.

Everyone seemed to want to see the baby. Eventually Traci had to remind everyone what a long day it had been and that she wanted Caitlin to sleep.

Sandra bustled about, helping in every way she could; trying to make things easier for the family.

"Sandra, you've done all you can do. Sit down. You must be exhausted. People are going to think I'm a slave driver or something. You know you can stay the night if you'd like?"

"Are you sure?"

"Of course I'm sure. I wouldn't have asked if I wasn't. Besides, we still haven't talked about whatever it is you have to tell me."

"Right you are and that is absolutely a must."

"Really?"

"Really."

"Is Bill working this week?"

"Probably. He's in the process of selling Satellite so lately it's hard to tell when he's going into the office and when he's not."

"Darren and Preston are going to join us when we talk."

"Us too," Sebastian chimed in, with Angelika at his side.

"All of this sounds so ominous. Does it have anything to do with the state of things uptown?"

"That's just the tip of the iceberg," Sebastian added.

"What do you know about this?"

"Traci, we'll talk, but not here."

As soon as Bill approached, everyone changed the subject. Traci was dumbfounded.

"What's this, a family meeting, and no one invited me?"

"We were just discussing whether or not mother had any affairs we need to get in order."

"Oh."

"Traci, some people are leaving. They wanted to say good-bye."

"I'll be right there."

Bill eventually did return to work two days later. It was just in time, because Sebastian and Angelika had flight plans for the next day.

They waited until they were sure Bill was gone and Sebastian, Angelika, Sandra, Preston and Darren gathered together in the living room to speak to Traci.

Sandra started things off. "Traci, have you ever heard of a Supreme Court case called Loving v. Virginia?"

"It does sound familiar."

"The Lovings were an interracial married couple who were criminally charged under a Virginia statute banning such marriage. With the help of the ACLU, the Lovings filed suit seeking to overturn the law. In 1967, the Supreme Court ruled in their favor, striking down the Virginia statute and all state anti-miscegenation laws as unconstitutional violations of the Fourteenth Amendment."

"I do remember hearing about that couple but I still don't understand. If the Supreme Court ruled in their favor, what, close to sixty years ago, why is this something we're talking about now?"

"Because as we speak The Executive Branch is in the process of putting things in place to obstruct the decision in Loving v. Virginia."

"And you know what follows after that?" said Preston. "Did you know that in 2003 the U.S. Supreme Court ruled that Texas could not stop people of the same sex from engaging in sexual activity? However, The Texas Penal Code still states that it is a Class C misdemeanor to engage in *deviate sexual intercourse with another individual of the same sex*. Ironically, all of this is stated right after a line explaining that the law is unconstitutional."

"Darren...and Preston, why don't you move back here? Leave the South. I never thought that was the place for you anyway, Darren."

"Traci, it's bigger than that. This is stretching outside the country. We've already heard rumblings in Germany as well," Sebastian added.

"It's the Civil War all over again. However, I'm afraid this time the odds are stacked even greater against us," Sandra said.

Darren got up and walked across the room. "I refuse to believe that. I, for one, plan to fight until my last breath."

"That's why they're constantly on our tails," Sandra said.

"What do you mean?'

"Did you see the strange-looking guy today with the top hat and trench coat?"

"Yeah, I was going to ask you about him, but when I turned around, you were all gone."

"That's what we do; try to stay one step ahead of guys like that. They are sent to keep an eye on us. Sometimes, they're even sent to kill us, depending on how large of a threat we're considered. They guy today was probably watching and reporting back."

"About what?"

"Who was in attendance," Sandra said. "Or, whether or not anything was said that might qualify as a threat to anyone of any importance."

"They also do it in the hopes that they'll frighten enough people away. I'm pretty sure that was the intent today. That guy had an audience. That's the reason for the somber dress and the staring. It's their goal to unnerve as many people as they can. And I see it worked," Preston said.

"You haven't heard anything until I tell you what one of the COC's forensic people believe was unearthed near the Washington Hilton. After POTUS and the V.P. were killed, there was all this speculation about why no one had heard anything at all from either of their wives. Bones were found, along with a brooch. And the brooch bears a striking resemblance to one worn by the First Lady. It's incredible when you think that in an age of such technology, that all this information could be so easily covered up. I guess the media is just as worried as everyone else. No one wants to risk being killed or having their families killed. I remember a time when journalists didn't give a damn about who got mad or who wanted to quash a story. The story was told regardless. Now, everything is under wraps," said Darren.

Traci couldn't tell a lie. She was unnerved. She wasn't sure why the guy was there or whether his presence had anything at all to do with her and her family or not. Now, at least, she knew the truth. "If all of this is true, what can we do?"

"We're already doing it. Every day we help more and more people. There are families out there that are suffering."

"You mean like my mother was?" Traci asked.

"I hate to minimize what your mother was going through, but yes. Women and children are especially vulnerable. There are single women working in homes just so their children can have a roof over their heads, then some sicko swoops in and decides he can take whatever it is he wants and do whatever it is he wants, simply because these women are desperate. Whenever possible, we try to discourage our members from taking live-in positions for food and shelter. It sounds like a good idea in theory, but it seldom is." Sandra paused for a moment and sighed. "Then there are the police, who try to get family and friends to turn each other in. Often, the incentives offered are never supplied, so you have people racked with guilt for turning a friend or a loved one in and not even getting anything out of it."

"Well, baby girl," Darren interjected. "The first thing you can do is get your husband to stop contributing to the campaign of the man most anxious to see these plans come to fruition."

CHAPTER TWENTY-FOUR

"Bill, are you telling me you knew nothing about the politician whose campaign you are contributing to?"

Bill put his paper down on the kitchen table and folded his hands in front of him. "Nothing at all."

"I find that so hard to believe. You're the man that reads everything ten times to make sure all the I's are dotted and the T's are crossed. How could you not know? All I did was a simple Google search and it was all spelled out there in black and white. He's a really bad guy."

Bill glared at Traci. "You believe everything you read on the Internet?"

"So what, now you're defending him? I thought you knew nothing about him. It was just something I read on the Internet. I watched a YouTube video of him when he was governor of Texas and he did everything short of saying black people should be back in chains and leg irons. What he did say loud and clear was that he believed that blacks and whites should not marry; he was talking about us. I mean, do you get that? He's talking about us. He's also talking about our baby girl, sleeping peacefully upstairs; that little girl that we made. A man like him considers Caitlin, and children like her, to be an abomination. Are you okay with that?"

Bill stood up to go fix himself another cup of coffee by the stove. "You know that I'm not."

Traci followed him and stood beside him. "So, how did your name end up on a list of contributors to his campaign?"

"My best guess would be that it has something to do with my mother or Satellite."

Traci looked him in the eyes. "I thought Satellite was being sold?"

Bill avoided her stare. "It's in the process of being sold, but it's not sold yet. You don't understand, Traci. I have a staff of about two hundred people that handle every aspect of what it takes to make the company run. I don't handle every miniscule detail. There's a department for everything, including contributions."

"Why would there be a department for that? Political contributions aren't even deductible."

"Traci, I'm tired, my stress level is at an all-time high, and the last thing I want to do tonight is argue about a contribution I might or might not have made."

Shortly after dinner, Bill went to bed while Tracy stayed up, watching television in the living room. She fell asleep on the couch and only got up once to feed Caitlin. By the time she decided to get in bed, Bill was already up and getting ready for work. It was the first night in a long time the two of them hadn't slept in the same bed together.

After their mother passed away, Traci, Darren and Sebastian decided that, given all of the circumstances, they had to maintain as much contact with one another as possible. In addition to learning of Bill's campaign contributions, Traci learned that everyone close to her was a member of the COC. She was surprised to find out that there was even a chapter in Germany.

Traci continued to research more and more about what she had learned from Darren, Sebastian and Sandra and the new information she had discovered on her own. Over time, she became more and more aware of what was going on around her and started sending information to Sandra until Sandra warned her. One day they were having lunch and Traci mentioned that the emails she was sending her kept coming back as undeliverable.

"That's another reason why you should join the group," Sandra said. "We have members from all sectors. There are computer experts, members of government; teachers; lawyers. You name it, we've got it. Once you're a member there are all sorts of protocols in place to help protect its members from harm."

"So, you admit, there's danger involved in being a member of the group?"

"Traci, you've learned enough to know, we are living in troubling times. We're all in danger. We're in danger of losing the basic human rights we've come to depend upon. Hell, some already have. I met with a family last week that was being kept in horrible living conditions. The youngest child was only three months old. They came to work for this family because neither the husband nor the wife could find work and since food stamps and public assistance are now a thing of the past, they had to go live with this rich couple.

"The wife only wanted them to work for her because she needed the woman to act as wet nurse and the husband saw an opportunity to fuel his sick fetishes. No one was safe from him; the kids, the wife, even the husband. We got them out. That family will probably be damaged their entire lives, but at least they are away from that couple.

"I hear and see stories like this all the time and it's getting worse each day. The moment people were stripped of the ability to reach out and get aid, the sickness of the world took hold with even greater force. But, I can't decide for you. You have to make up your mind on your own. Especially given your circumstances."

Traci was confused. "What circumstances?"

Sandra sighed heavily. "Have you forgotten that you're married to a white man? A white man that was contributing to the campaign of the man we're trying to overthrow. If that bastard becomes President, we're all slaves again and I'm not speaking meta-phorically."

Three days later Traci was a member of the group. She was surprised to find that there were just as many white members as there were black. When she mentioned what she noticed to another member, he explained to her that their mission was not about racial division. The group was about maintaining racial equality. Traci believed in the organization and was now much more com-fortable with her decision to join.

All of the information the organization had gathered over the years was available for viewing by its members. Traci sought out the list of campaign contributors and found that Bill had been contributing to the Republican candidate's campaign from the start. It was unnerving. What was even more unnerving was the fact that when a new all-inclusive list was compiled of new and old contributors, somehow Bill's name had vanished from the list.

"How could this be?" Traci asked one of the members responsible for compiling the list.

"It's simple. Typically, the list will include everyone's name on it. Most people assume that no one pays close attention to the names on those lists. But a few select people and organizations do. What some don't realize when they quickly go about getting their name removed from a list is that the old list is still floating around someplace and with us, it's not just floating around. We keep every single list, every single piece of paper we've ever compiled. We have to. This whole thing is so insidious, we need every tool at our disposal to try our very best to stay ahead of the treachery."

"You make it sound like a game."

"It is a game. It's no different than chess. Just like chess, it requires the contemplation of both players using both tactical maneuvers and strategic planning, with the ultimate goal of capturing the King. The only difference in our case is we're playing to ensure that the King doesn't capture us."

Traci finally realized that everything she had been told, everything she had been reading about, might be about to come true. Her daughter had recently turned two years old. She realized if she had been a lot less complacent she might have thought twice about bringing a child into this world. By the time she made her way home all those thoughts were lost. Her little girl, walking toward her calling her Mommy, was all she needed to remind her that no matter what kind of world they were living in, her daughter was not a mistake. She was a beauty to behold and everything she was fighting for was for her.

"Where have you been?" Bill asked.

"Out with Sandra," she lied.

"Really?"

"Yes."

"Are you sure you weren't on Jennings Street, in the Bronx?" he asked as he flipped over a hamburger in a frying pan, preparing their dinner.

"What!" Traci was so shocked and appalled by the admission that he knew exactly where she was that she didn't even try to make up a lie. "Are you having me followed?"

Then she remembered that time years earlier, when her mother had first fallen sick. Suddenly Bill was there at some out of the way diner she and Darren had picked specifically because it was in a remote place. Yet, Bill was there, standing at the window, as if he knew exactly where she would be.

"You've done this before, haven't you? You've been following me for years. Haven't you? Why? What reason would you have to keep tabs on me? This isn't normal behavior. Normal husbands don't have their wives followed for no reason."

"Clearly, it is for a reason. That little organization you were hanging out with thinks they're so obscure, but everyone knows who they are and what they are. You are putting all of us in danger by spending time with them. And, I hope you weren't stupid enough to actually join them."

All Traci heard was the word stupid. "Stupid! Stupid! That's what you've always thought of me, isn't it? That I'm some stupid woman that you can manipulate? Just tell me one thing. Why on earth did you marry me? Was this part of your involvement with your President-elect, slave trader?"

"I don't know what they have been filling your head with, but right now you sound like a mad woman."

Traci went and stood beside him at the stove. "Oh, I'm the mad woman? Aren't you the one that's been following me, or have you been having me followed? Which is it? Never mind; I don't even want to know."

Bill realized things were headed down an irreversible path and tried to correct it.

"Traci, all I'm trying to do here is protect my family. Many of these people that they are trying to crush are friends of my mother's. They've known me since I was a baby. What you're involved in, I'm involved in. There's no way to escape it. These people consider that organization a threat and they're going to fight just as hard to crush the COC as the COC is fighting to crush them. I end up smack-dab in the middle of it all if you're involved. So, do you get why I've had you followed?"

"I get it, but I don't like it and I can't help but see you in a different light based on what you've just told me."

"You're not by yourself. I saw you in a different light when I found out you were consorting with this group. This is the same organization that tried to link me to a terrorist act. What do you think would have happened to me if that had worked? I could have been arrested and God only knows what else."

"Only if you were guilty."

"Do you really believe that?"

"Yes, as a matter of fact I do?"

"So, how does that explain all of the people that went to prison for crimes that they didn't commit?"

"Nothing is a perfect science. But, usually, if it walks like a duck, talk likes a duck and quacks like a duck, it's a duck."

While Bill and Traci were in the kitchen talking, Caitlin was watching cartoons on the television in the living room. Both Traci and Bill heard the broadcast interruption and rushed into the living room. They didn't need to hear the report. The topic was splashed across the screen in big bold letters: *1967 SUPREME COURT DECISION OVERTURNED: INTERRACIAL MARRIAGE ONCE AGAIN DEEMED UNLAWFUL.*

CHAPTER TWENTY-FIVE

"Did you know this was coming?" Traci asked Bill, pacing the floor. "Well, did you?"

"We all did, Traci. I know just about as much as you do and we all knew this was coming. That's why I've been trying to get you to keep a low profile. They will come looking for anyone who violates this law. And, now, thanks to your involvement with that militant group, that includes us, as well as Caitlin."

"What do you mean, Caitlin? She hasn't broken any laws?"

"You can't really be that naïve. Of course children like Caitlin will suffer in some way or another. Laws like these were created in the first place to discourage mixing of the races. Children like Caitlin are living, breathing proof that their belief system has been challenged."

"Please stop saying 'children like Caitlin.' She's my daughter, not some thing."

"Have you forgotten that she's my daughter, too?"

"Then why don't you act like it?"

Traci considered leaving Bill and taking Caitlin with her, but she still loved him and he was Caitlin's father. Not only that, where would she go? The COC thought she would be safer and do more good for the organization if she stayed where she was.

It took some time, but both Traci and Bill settled back in to some level of comfort with one another. Traci, of course, was careful not to openly associate with the organization ever again and confined her communication with them to carefully planned interactions. The only time she mentioned the COC to Bill was when Preston Chambers was arrested.

"Darren's friend, Preston, was arrested today."

"On what charges?" Bill asked.

"They are calling it treason. Apparently, it is being claimed that Preston and some of the other members of the COC were offering assistance to members of al-Qaeda."

"Aren't you glad you didn't join when I advised against it?"

"Yeah, a lot of good it did. I'm a prisoner in my own home."

"You're a lot better off than some. One of my coworkers married an African woman from Eritrea. The young people there are forced to serve in military camps for years. Thousands of these young people end up in refugee camps in Sudan. The women are raped and often held captive for years. Some of them have even had their kidneys removed without their permission. She escaped and now she's being sent back. Her husband is afraid they're going to kill her in Eritrea when she returns and he's probably right."

"Please tell me this isn't some sort of count your blessings speech. I'm glad I'm not in a military camp in Eritrea or a refugee camp in Sudan, but I'm also mad as hell that I'm every bit a prisoner as those women are." She paused. "I truly have no voice. My family members have no voice. We are all slaves. All of us except you and Angelika."

"Why did you mention Angelika? Is it because she's white?"

"Yes, it is. You and Angelika both can leave. You can leave me and Angelika can leave Sebastian and that will be the end of it. We are not so lucky. My life is altered forever. Everything I have is tied to you. I'm damned if I leave and I'm damned if I stay. And, so is Caitlin. But, I don't want to talk about this anymore. I don't have enough energy to fight."

"Is that what you think we are now; just two people who fight?"

"I haven't felt joyous in a really long time, Bill. How could I? How would you feel if you had to hide from the world? I can't even take my own daughter to the park anymore, or to play outside in our own garden. This is no kind of a life. But, it's not worth talking about; it is what it is." Traci stared into his eyes, trying to read his mind. "In the meantime, is there anything we can do for Preston?"

"Absolutely not. He was arrested for treason. Anyone who comes to his aid will be considered a supporter as well. If anyone does indeed try to help him, it should definitely not be us. We should keep a low profile until we can figure out a way to get out of the country. Despite what you might think, it doesn't fill me with any sort of pleasure to know that my wife has to live under these conditions. I've always wanted nothing but the best for you. All I've ever wanted was for you to be happy."

For a moment Traci softened and she remembered the Bill that she loved. The battle lines had been drawn such that it was difficult to tell the difference from enemy and friend. When it came to Bill, she was especially confused. There were so many indications that he could be either friend or foe. She knew getting help for Preston and Darren from Bill was a long shot so, instead, Traci decided to focus on Bill's plans.

"Where can we go?" she asked. "Sebastian says things are starting to get bad in Germany as well. They fired him from the airline, you know. He and Angelika are just as worried as we are."

"Yeah, they said it was cutbacks, but only the attendants of color were let go."

"None of us should ever forget that Germany has a history rooted in racism. The Nazi Holocaust, genocide, and Eugene Fisher."

"Eugene Fisher?" Bill said.

"Eugene Fisher was a German professor of medicine, anthropology and eugenics. He conducted horrible medical experiments on race. He would sterilize some, and inject others with diseases like smallpox and tuberculosis. He believed in genocide for so-called inferior races. Given all of that I don't think Germany is the place we run to."

The concerned look on Bill's face was unmistakable. "We'll figure something out," he said.

"What? What will we figure out?"

"I don't know yet, but there has to be some solution."

"What if there isn't? Every day I keep expecting the knock at the door. I'm amazed every day that someone hasn't told that I'm here. It wasn't so long ago that if someone had told me that inter-racial marriage would be outlawed, I would have told them they were crazy. It makes me wish I had been more politically active."

"What could you have done? The power it took to set these wheels into motion was far greater than anything a simple voter could have corrected."

"Bill, do you truly believe that? Sure, there was a point of no return, when things were so out of control that it was impossible to stop it, but what about ten years ago, or even twenty years ago? Complacency is what allowed this to happen. There was a time when we, the voters, had power. Unfortunately, we didn't exercise that power and that's why things are the way they are now. I can remember the exact moment when I realized things would never be the same. It was January 20, 2009. Only thing is I thought things were changing for the better.

"I was twenty-two years old and so full of hope. I had such an idealized view of America. I was so stupid. Little did I know it would take more than the election of the first black President of the United States to change the world, it would take pro-active involvement, as much and as often as possible. Sadly, it came in small degrees, but it wasn't enough. It was too little and I'm beginning to think, too late."

"This isn't the Traci I know talking."

"I thought this was the Traci you wanted. You don't want me to even utter the name COC. Yet, you say I'm not the Traci you know. Of course, I'm giving up. If I can't fight, what else can I do? That is the definition of fight or flight. I tried to fight and you and your people stripped me of the potential to do that. Now all that's left is flight."

"That's the first time I've ever heard you refer to me in those terms—*your people*? What does that mean, anyway? I always thought we were all the same. That we were all a part of the human race?"

"Correct me if I'm wrong, but in this little equality concept you got going here, which one of us can't look out the window or go outside? That would be me. So, I'm having a little bit of difficulty embracing this illusion of equality. I'm not equal at all. I'm a slave. I'm a prisoner. And, in case you've forgotten, so is your daughter."

"I can't do this anymore. I'm going to bed. Are you coming or not?"

"I guess I am," Traci whispered. "It'll be more difficult for anyone to see me in the bedroom."

Bill didn't hear what she had said or pretended not to hear and simply continued up the stairs to bed.

Traci turned on the television and curled up in a blanket on the floor.

Bill considered commenting on how silly Traci was being by choosing to sit on the floor rather than getting into bed with him, then it occurred to him that her action might not have been a way to show how angry she was but may have been because she was afraid of being seen by anyone. He got out of bed as well, dragging the blanket with him and wrapped it around the two of them.

"Traci, please, just tell me what to do. I love you and Caitlin more than anything, but I'm lost. I don't know what I'm supposed to do. You have to be the one. You have to tell me what it is I need to do."

"You're supposed to save us, Bill. I don't know how to tell you to do that. I only know the ways that I've considered. But as has been demonstrated, you and I are different, whether we want to admit it or not. The tools at your disposal are different than mine. Only you know what those tools are and how to use them to achieve the desired effect."

Both Bill and Traci fell asleep on the floor in each other's arms. When Bill woke up, both Traci and Caitlin were gone. He wondered if she had left for good. He even searched the house for a note. There was nothing. For the first time since this all got started Bill cried. He was sure that Traci and Caitlin were gone and convinced that he deserved the pain that he was in.

"Oh, Mommy, it's the park."

It had been so long since she had been able to take her daughter to a park, Traci was so happy to have found it. It was similar to a compound, but there was so much space for the children to run and be happy. It even felt good for Traci to be able to be around other adults. Since everything had gotten underway her world had slipped into a very tiny nucleus that included Bill and Caitlin. Here there were all kinds of people. It was almost normal.

A good-looking black gentleman approached Traci. "Your first time here?" he asked.

"Yeah, it is. I didn't know anything about this place. I'm so glad my daughter has a place she can play and be a kid."

"I know what you mean. My son is an only child and I worry

about him so much. He never complains but he must miss running and playing and just being a boy."

"Yeah, my daughter is an only child, too. Which one is yours?" Traci asked.

"The redhead over there."

Traci laughed. "You mean the little boy who is playing with my little girl. Isn't that ironic?"

"You know why, don't you?" the gentleman asked.

"No, not really. Why?"

"Just look at them. With the exception that my son's hair is red and your daughter's is blonde, they could be sister and brother."

"Wow, you're right. They do look a lot alike."

Traci enjoyed talking to another adult that wasn't her husband and the man she was speaking with seemed to enjoy it as well. Living under the circumstances they were forced to live under was no easy task, especially when there was no one to talk to all day but your children.

"How'd you find this place?" he asked.

"A friend told me about it. I was climbing the walls, being cooped up all the time. If I was older, it might be a little easier to lounge around all the time, but I was always so active. Now, I find myself pacing the floors just to be able to have something to do. I wish I could do this every day, but I realize it's impossible."

"They tell us to vary our routines and to not come the same days of the week. It's for our own safety. I'm so preoccupied sometimes I forget what day I came or didn't come."

"Same here. I really have to vary my routine. My husband doesn't want me to have anything to do with any of these organizations. I almost have to hide what I'm doing, but I figured out since I've been sitting here that I'm going to come clean. My daughter and I both need this."

"You're probably right. I've noticed that my son, Jacob, sleeps much more soundly at night on the days when he comes here."

"Caitlin as well. I guess it makes sense. They've got all that energy and nothing to do with it. Just look at them. They haven't stopped running since they got here. You'll be back again, won't you?"

"I'm sure I will. I don't think I'll be able to keep Jacob away."

"Can I ask you a personal question?" Traci said.

"Fire away," he said.

"Where is Jacob's mother?"

"His mother was never the motherly type. So, when all this got started, she didn't give it a second thought. She was gone, lickety-split."

"All of this gets so frustrating sometimes, but I can't imagine being without Caitlin. I would die without her."

"Same thing with me and Jacob. So, you're still married? How is that going, things being what they are? Do you ever resent him?"

"Do I ever! Hell, I resent him all the time. I have to constantly remind myself not to be so angry with him. It's hard, though, because when I look at him, he represents something now that he didn't represent before. I tell him all the time, it feels like I'm his prisoner."

"It was so nice talking to you," he said as he left. "Jacob! It's time to go. Bye, ladies. Hope to see you again."

An hour later, Traci returned with Caitlin, excited and happy. They were both wearing some sort of makeup. For Caitlin it simply made her look a bit lighter than her usual skin tone and it was the first time Bill realized that Caitlin really could pass for white. Traci also had applied some foundation to her skin. On her it was only passable along with the hoodie she was wearing. For Traci it was just enough to allow her to do what she set out to do.

"Bill, I know you told me to stay away from the COC, but I

made a choice this morning. I was sick of feeling like a prisoner in this house and I felt even sicker knowing that Caitlin had to be a prisoner as well, so I went to one of the compounds that the group keeps. It's secluded and has plenty of outdoor space and it allows children like Caitlin and women and men like me the freedom to spend time with others like us."

"You said women and men?"

"Yes, did it really never occur to you that there are some men in the same position as me? There are just as many black men out there that married white women and are hiding in plain sight. In fact, after going there today, I think there might be more men than there are women."

"Really? Is that where you heard that term, hiding in plain sight?"

"Yeah, it's catchy, isn't it? H.I.P.S. Hips, is what they call themselves. I like it. I like them. It was the first time I saw Caitlin *really* act like a kid in a long time."

"Daddy, guess what? Mommy and I went to the park today and we got on the swings and there was a jungle gym and I got to hit a softball with a big plastic bat!"

"Really, sweet pea."

"Yeah, it was fun!"

"Would you like to go back there?"

"Yeah! Can you go with us next time?"

"I don't know, honey. Why don't you ask Mom?"

"Mom, can he? Can Daddy go with us to our special park? It's a secret, but Daddy can know our secrets. Right?"

"Right, baby. Daddy can know all of our secrets, baby."

Traci was more relaxed than she had been in quite some time. She talked with Bill into the wee hours of the morning. It was her hope that he would understand why it was so important for her to remain connected to groups like H.I.P.S. She needed it. Caitlin needed it. Otherwise, Traci knew neither she nor Caitlin would survive. Not only that, her marriage to Bill would never survive.

After they stayed up all night talking and drinking wine, Traci and Bill made love for the first time in a long time. It brought back such pleasant memories.

Traci was moaning so loudly she put her fingers in her mouth to mute the noise. Her head rolled back and forth across the pillow and she was happy to see that they had not lost desire for one another.

Except for the brand new black curtains and matching black blinds that hung on the windows, the same curtains and blinds he had purchased for Caitlin's room, meant to conceal their existence.

Traci wondered how much the black curtains and shades really kept out. Nearby, were the same neighbors she had said good morning and good night to, far too often to count. Traci wondered what their thoughts were. Did they believe she had left or that she was arrested for breaking the law? Or, were they the kind of neighbors that wanted nothing more than to mind their own business? There had been so many times since she had had to hide out that she searched her memories trying to remember whether or not she had ever pissed any of them off. She always tried to be a good neighbor wherever she lived. But, you never knew when the simplest thing could annoy someone and when presented with an opportunity just like this one, they would exercise their power. That was something even thick black curtains and black blinds couldn't cover.

Traci took one quick peek past the blinds just in time to see Mr. Wittingham walking his very friendly cocker spaniel. As much as Traci used to complain about that dog jumping on her when she was on her way to work, she wished Rosey would jump on her one last time, wagging her tail like she was her very best friend.

CHAPTER TWENTY-SIX

Many believed that Bryan had either left the country or been killed. In fact he had done both. After an especially bad beating by the cops one night, Bryan faked his death, hoping that if no one knew he was alive, no one would look for him. It didn't take long for all of its members, including Bryan, to learn that membership in the COC was like a bull's eye on your back if anyone found out.

So, when Bryan was convinced everyone believed he was dead, he made his way to Mexico and he probably would have been fine hiding out in the remote village of Emiliano Zapata for a couple more years, except he couldn't get Traci out of his mind. He found ways to keep up with her life and make sure that she was safe. But, he was concerned that she would never be safe as long as she was with Bill. Not only because he was a white man, but also because Bryan believed that Bill didn't possess the strength required to survive the long haul. News that there was a traitor in the COC got to Bryan and when he found out Traci's brother was involved, he knew he would have to find a way to get word to not only Darren but Traci as well.

Traci noticed someone watching her and Caitlin immediately. She now visited the H.I.P.S. compound at least once a week. She tried to vary the routine of which day of the week she showed up, just in case. But, she thought she owed it to Caitlin to try to give her an opportunity to laugh and play like normal kids. After all, it wasn't her idea to be born into the world she was in. That was all her mommy and daddy's idea. Traci shifted position, hoping to get a better look at the hooded figure watching them and to conceal her own appearance. Just when she thought it was impossible to figure out who or what was under the person's hood, he got up and appeared to be heading directly for her. At first she was afraid and pulled Caitlin close to her, then suddenly she realized there was something familiar about the walk.

"After all these years, you mean to tell me you don't recognize me?"

"Bryan! What are you doing here? Darren told me you were killed."

"Well, rumors of my death were greatly exaggerated. As you can see, I am alive and well."

Traci touched the side of his face. "What's that?"

"Oh, that ole thing? That's nothing but battle scars; a little something to tell my grandkids."

Traci looked around. "Are they here?" she asked.

"Is who here?"

"Your kids, of course."

"I don't have any kids; at least not yet. Why, are you applying for the job?"

"You're still shameless. Stop flirting with me. So, if you don't have any kids, what are you doing here? This is a compound for parents with young children. How did you get in?"

"I told them I was here to take you away from all of this."

"Would you stop playing around Bryan? Now, why are you here?"

"Darren might be in a little bit of trouble. That boy he's been playing around with; there are some that believe he may in fact be a traitor. Someone's been leaking information and just about every-one I've talked to is sure it's Preston Chambers."

"I knew there was something about that asshole I didn't like."

"Whew, get angry much?" Bryan asked, jokingly.

"Being a prisoner in your own home will do that to a person."

"How long do you think you can do that?" Bryan asked.

"I have no idea. It's just a matter of time before someone knocks on, or worse yet, breaks down our door. I'm worried for myself, but I'm twice as worried about Caitlin. I don't even know what happens with children like her when their mother is arrested. Would they even let her stay with Bill?"

"No, they would not. I'm not just saying that because I'd like you to run away with me. I'm saying it because it's true. First of all, if they come to your door, they already know that any child in that house is multiracial and that's all they need to know. And, even if they don't come to your door, Caitlin isn't white enough to pass for white, even with the makeup. I would have been able to tell even if I didn't know who her mother and father were."

"Really? I was so sure my baby could pass. I hoped she could because that would mean if I thought they were getting close, I might just turn myself in and let her stay here with Bill. Then, they would have to prove her mother was black if they even knew. Or, Bill could simply run away with her someplace where no one ever even heard of Traci Sanders Bianco."

"That's not going to work. Besides, your daughter needs her mother. Who else is going to teach her only the things a woman can teach her?"

"It's nice to hear it from someone else. Most of the time it's so hard to think of letting her go that I start to believe that I'm just being selfish."

"It's okay to be selfish when it comes to loving your child. This world is topsy-turvy. Things are not supposed to be like this. Love between two people shouldn't be regulated by law. When this first happened, I kept thinking there would be such an uprising that it would all end with little more than a whimper. Fooled the hell out of me."

"You ain't the only one. I always believed we were invincible. I thought of us as a people as such fearless creatures. Then, it finally dawned on me that we only made up fourteen percent of the entire United States population. Many of us may in fact be quite heroic, but the numbers just ain't there. It's the Spartans versus the Persians all over again," Traci added.

"So, have you been in touch with that brother of yours?"

"Here and there, but nothing substantive. Every now and then I'll get a call from some number I don't recognize and it will be him."

"Are you still using the same cell phone? Girl, you can't do that. If they're looking for you, that's how they're going to find you."

"Point taken."

"So, what's Bill's stand on all this?"

"What stand?"

"I figured as much."

"What is that supposed to mean?" Traci asked.

"It means that when the chips are down, he's not going to save you or your daughter."

"Are you sure you're not a little bit prejudiced when it comes to Bill? You know, him being the man that came after you and all?"

"Not at all. I'm doing what I've always done; looking out for your best interest."

"Oh, is that what you've done? Is that what you were doing when you were pounding out my bed springs with Ms. Jennifer?"

"We are knee deep in a cataclysm and you're still bringing up one roll in the hay I had with Jennifer. Women; you have memories like elephants."

"No you didn't just use the women line on me? I remember there was a time when you said I wasn't like any other woman you knew. My how times change."

"Quite the contrary, that hasn't changed at all. In fact, I now believe that even more than I did before. You most certainly are special, Sunshine. Otherwise, you wouldn't have survived as long as you have."

"Wow, Bryan, way to scare a girl."

"I'm not trying to scare you, just giving you big ups! You're a trooper. I have no reason to believe that you won't continue to survive. You have to. Because I have decided that I am going to marry you one day, just like I always planned."

Traci simply laughed. "And, on that note, it's time to take Caitlin home to her father."

"If you hear from Darren, give him this number," Bryan said, handing Traci a piece of paper.

"I thought you told me not to use the same phone?"

"I don't use the same phone," said Bryan. "I have several phones that I keep switching back and forth and eventually as I add new ones to the repertoire I throw some of them away. You can't let technology bring you down. Cell phones and emails are the quickest way to do that if you're on the run."

"Are you?"

"Huh?"

"Are you on the run?" Traci asked.

"Hell yeah. Anybody that was ever a member of the group long enough for anyone of danger to find out about it is on the run. That's why you're on the run? Even though you weren't a member for long, most of your friends and family were members long enough to make up for it. The moment you joined you were on their hit list, because they had already seen your face enough times, long before you officially joined. You were already associated with the group."

"That sounds like something Bill said."

"I never said he wasn't a smart man. I just said he wasn't a courageous man."

"Be nice, Bryan."

"I am being nice. In fact, I'm probably the nicest guy you know."

Just as Bryan was stepping close enough to kiss Traci, Caitlin came running over from the slide.

"Mommy, I'm cold."

"Okay, baby. We're leaving now."

"Can we come back tomorrow?" Caitlin asked.

"Maybe not tomorrow, Sweetie, but we will come back another day."

"Yay!" Caitlin watched Bryan walking away with much curiosity. "Mommy, who was that man?"

"Just another man at the park. That's all, honey. Just another man at the park."

Caitlin was exhausted by the time they got home and so was Traci. She curled up on the bed with Caitlin and Caitlin talked all about her day and how much she enjoyed it. For some reason she was happy that Bill wasn't home. That was the thing about feeling like a prisoner. If you were a prisoner, someone had to represent the Prison Warden. The only person that could represent that position was Bill. He was the only adult there, besides Traci. It also occurred to Traci that maybe she wasn't missing Bill because she had seen Bryan. Both Caitlin and Traci fell asleep. Caitlin dreamed of a life in which every day was spent going to her special park and Traci dreamed of a life in which she was sure without a doubt she was with the man of her choice because she truly wanted to be and not because she had to be.

CHAPTER TWENTY-SEVEN

*T*hanks to connections he still had at the COC, Bryan was able to connect with Darren. They set a time and Bryan called at exactly the time they had set.

"Man, I thought I had hiding down to an art form, but you are the King of hiding," Bryan said.

"I have to be," Darren replied. "They are hot on my trail, like a motherfucker. You would think I was Public Enemy Number One."

"I guess in their eyes you are. After all, you were one of the group's first members. I still think of you as our fearless leader. You made most of the connections and you were instrumental in bringing in most of the members. If it weren't for you, we wouldn't have even the small level of power we have now."

"What power?" Darren asked. "What have we really accomplished? People are still dying, women and children are still being exposed to the very worst atrocities. I feel like we've accomplished nothing."

"Don't give in to that way of thinking. Even if you have to go someplace and hide out like I had to do, do that. At least then you'll live to fight another day. I refuse to believe this is our destiny. It can't be. Just like our ancestors got out from under the thumbs of their oppressors, eventually we will do the same."

"Do you really believe that?"

"Yes, as a matter of fact I do. Not only that, I *have* to believe it. If not, what else do I have?"

"I guess you're right."

"I know I'm right."

"You can always come back with me to Mexico."

"Is that where you were?"

"Hell yeah. The people there ask no questions. And, a little bit of money goes a long way."

Darren sighed. "I'll keep that in mind."

"I'll tell you why I called, though," Bryan said. "How much do you know about your man Preston?"

"Preston? Why?"

"There's been some talk that he was one of the people leaking information. Not only that, there are those that believe that was how he was released so quickly."

"No. I know Preston. We've been together for a while. He's been one of the organization's staunchest supporters."

"He would have to be, wouldn't he, in order to gain everyone's trust, including yours. Think about it. He was being held for treason. The prison is full of those falsely accused of treason, but somehow Preston was able to get released within a matter of weeks with not so much as a scratch on him. How do you think he got out?" Bryan asked.

"How do you know he didn't have a scratch on him?" Darren asked.

"That's been the talk. I have my connections. I got to tell you, man, given everything I've heard, I don't trust him. I'm just telling you to be careful. Okay?"

"Okay, I will. So, have you seen my sister?"

"Why do you ask?"

"Because I know you and there is no way in hell you came all the way back from your safe comfortable spot in Mexico for me."

"I'm hurt, man. That you would think I have an ulterior motive hurts me deeply."

"So, she still looks good, doesn't she?"

"Hella hot!"

They both fell out in laughter over the phone.

"I can't believe your crazy, lovesick ass is still carrying a torch for my sister. My fugitive sister, who's married to a rich white man. If that ain't love, I don't know what is."

"I'm working on a five-year plan. Within five years I'm going to win her back."

"Five-year plan? What about those ten years that already passed?"

"Those years don't mean a thing. I was giving her a chance to miss me. And, look what happened; the fates conspired to give me an opportunity to win her back."

"Please, explain that one. I can't wait to hear this logic."

"I look at it this way; if we hadn't been faced with this devastating cataclysm we find ourselves engulfed in, she would be living her nice, safe, comfortable life with her rich husband and there would be no reason to question her choices. I bet you she's questioning her choices now. I can bet you if right now she was given the choice of marrying a man that cheated on her once and marrying a man that meant she had to hide from the world, possibly for the rest of her life, she would choose *me*, the man that cheated once."

"Good luck with that, Bryan. You obviously don't know as much about my sister as I thought you did or women in general, for that matter."

"Fuck you, Darren."

"Promises, promises."

"That is so nasty. Don't ever say anything like that to me again. I'm standing here right now about to puke."

"You know you like it. I'll turn your ass out so bad, you'll be saying what woman."

They both chuckled.

"Hanging up now!" Bryan exclaimed.

"Bye, baby."

"Pew, pew, now my ears are bleeding."

"Later!"

"Later."

Darren thought long and hard about his discussion with Bryan. It was difficult for him to believe that the man that he had not only shared his dreams with, but his bed with, could be a traitor to the organization that he thought meant so much to both of them. He wondered if Preston was really capable of betraying him.

"All you have to do is tell them where she is," said Preston.

"She's my sister. I'd die before turning her in. Have you forgotten about Caitlin? What about her?"

"That child is damn near white. She's light enough to pass. Her father's white. All he would have to do is tell people he was a widower and let Caitlin pass."

"Do you realize what you're saying? You're asking me to give the approval to kill my own sister in order to save us. I'm a lot of things, but I've never been a coward."

"No one's asking you to be a coward. These are difficult times and no one would fault you for doing everything you can to survive. It's just a matter of time before they find her anyway and you didn't really think she was going to be able to stay with Caitlin, did you?"

"Preston, my sister and I have always been strong and we've always had each other's backs. You can talk until you're blue in the face, but I'll never turn her in. I believe in her will and strength to survive this, as I do my own. I'm never giving up and Traci won't either."

"I hear where you're coming from, but what about me? I'm not strong like you and your sister. What am I supposed to do? I'm scared."

"As long as we've got each other, we'll be fine," Darren assured him.

"That's bullshit! The two of us haven't got a chance. We're black, we're gay and we're poor. I'm amazed we've survived this long."

"That's exactly the point I'm trying to make, Preston. We have survived on sheer will, determination and strength. We can't give up now."

"I'm not suggesting that we give up. All I'm saying is, maybe we need to use *all* of the resources we have available. Traci is going to be found out one way or another. Why shouldn't we benefit from it?"

"Do you hear the way that you sound? If you're going to take that stand, then Traci could just as easily turn us in!"

"How do you know she's not planning to? How do you even know she hasn't done it already?"

"Because I know my sister!"

"I hope you're right, because if you're not, you could be gambling with both our lives."

Darren used one of the many prepaid phones he had stockpiled. He had to warn Traci. He had no intention of ever turning his sister in, but he couldn't speak for Preston.

"Baby girl, I can't talk long, but if there is someplace you can go to, please do it now. They're getting closer. It's just a matter of time before they get to you and your family. Always know that I love you very much and stay safe."

CHAPTER TWENTY-EIGHT

Pictures of Darren, badly beaten, and obviously dead, arrived in the mail, addressed to Bill.

"Traci, I have something to show you. Let's go in the bathroom. I don't want Caitlin to see it."

"What is it?

"I'm so sorry I have to show you this, baby."

Traci took one look at the picture of her brother's face, beaten to a pulp, and collapsed to the floor. Behind the first photograph were other pictures at various angles. In one Darren was hanging from a tree with a noose around his neck. In another someone had done something so horrible to him with what appeared to be a mop or a broom handle.

"What kind of people are these? Who would do something like this? They're animals."

Darren wasn't the only person photographed hanging from trees. There were others. Too many others to even count. It reminded her of that old song Billy Holiday used to sing. Traci sat there on the floor, singing that song, over and over again.

Southern trees bear a strange fruit,
Blood on the leaves and blood at the root,
Black bodies swinging in the southern breeze,
Strange fruit hanging from the poplar trees,

If this had been normal times, this would have been the point when Bill took Traci to a doctor. It was obvious she was having a nervous breakdown. He felt even more helpless when Caitlin began knocking on the door looking for her mother.

"Mommy! Mommy! Are you in there?"

Bill left Traci in the bathroom and closed the door behind him.

"Mommy's using the bathroom right now. What do you need, sweetheart?"

"I wanted Mommy to sing me a song."

Bill tried to sing the *Mommies and Daddies* song he had always heard Traci sing to Caitlin when she couldn't get to sleep, but the chilling lyrics and melody of the song he had heard Traci singing wouldn't leave his head. Bill thought he had heard the song before, but the disparaging lyrics were something he was sure he would have remembered.

As hard as he tried, Bill could not convince Traci to leave the bathroom. She wouldn't talk, wouldn't respond. She wouldn't even get up off the floor. She kept singing those same lyrics over and over and over again.

Southern trees bear a strange fruit,
Blood on the leaves and blood at the root,
Black bodies swinging in the southern breeze,
Strange fruit handing from the poplar trees,

Eventually, when Bill was sure he wouldn't be able to take hearing those lyrics one more time, he slapped Traci, hard, across the face and she began to laugh hysterically. He almost wished she would go back to singing. That's when he got an idea that he hoped would work. He went into Caitlin's room, where she was now asleep. Picked her up in his arms and carried her, still asleep to the bathroom and laid her in Traci's arms. Within a matter of minutes Traci returned to normal, got up off the floor, laid Caitlin in her bed and curled up beside her daughter. She was asleep within a matter of moments. Bill assumed she was probably mentally exhausted. He decided it was imperative that he and his family get out of the country any way they could. If they didn't, Traci wasn't going to make it.

Bill pick up his cell phone and dialed.

"Mom, please help me. If we don't get out of here, Traci is not going to make it."

"I'll see what I can do," his mother responded.

For at least a week Bill's mother called in every favor she could think of; or at least every favor that wouldn't see them all arrested along with Traci. Finally, she called Bill with a possible solution.

"Both Traci and Caitlin are going to need passports."

"What about me?"

"You might be able to join them later, but you can't be seen traveling with them; not only for your safety, but for their safety as well. There's a guy down on Delancey Street that can get you passports and credit cards in Traci's new name."

"How do I find this guy?"

"He'll be wearing a purple hat."

"Really?"

"Really? What do you expect him to do, son, stand outside with a sign that reads fake passports and credit cards? I do believe I may have sheltered you too much."

"Mom, what are you talking about?"

"I spent so many years, trying to shelter you from the wrath of your father, I think I also sheltered you from learning about the world at large. You weren't prepared for any of this. You were especially not prepared for the life you chose for yourself. You would have been much better off marrying someone like Eleanor and leading a nice, safe life, like I suggested. You thought I was being a prying mother, when in fact, I saw the writing on the wall. You were never prepared for the spirited, stubborn, black woman you married. All of life's choices have consequences. Some of those consequences are obvious. To ignore the obvious is simply bad planning and will inevitably lead to pain and regret."

"I regret nothing, Mother; and the only pain I'm in is the pain associated with the world I find myself living in."

"I heard Traci mention once that she was ashamed of her complacency. No one has been more complacent than you have, son. What did you think you were doing when you contributed to the campaign of a man who made it crystal clear what his thoughts were on race-mingling?"

"But, Mother, you contributed as well."

"Yes, I did contribute and it wasn't because I am a racist, as I'm sure your wife and her friends and family believe. On the contrary, my contributions were to quiet long-standing rumors that somehow not only managed to survive the passage of time but a change in location as well. You see, son, you were not the first person to fall in love with someone black. His name was Leroy and he was beautiful. He worked for my parents and I don't think I've ever seen a more beautiful man before or since."

"Mother, what are you saying?"

"One night I was out on a date with one of the many jerks my mother and father had arranged for me and he decided he would have his way with me. I was young and didn't know half as many tricks as I know now. I was struggling to get away from him when Leroy saw me trying to get out of the car. You had to see him. He was about six-foot-four, arms the size of slabs of beef and a chest like stone. He pulled that four-eyed jerk out of that car and would have beaten him to a pulp if it weren't for me. The only reason I stopped him was because I didn't want Leroy to get into trouble. I would have like nothing more than to see him beat the living shit out of that asshole."

Bill listened to his mother, dumbfounded. He had never heard her talk this way. It was like he was meeting her for the very first time. "Mother, have you been drinking?"

"Yes, I have and quite a bit. Anyway, that night, I couldn't help myself. He was walking me home, it was dark out, the moon was shining and he was covered in sweat from tussling with ole four-eyes. So many days I had watched Leroy working with his shirt off, that Atlanta heat beaming down on him, and my mind would wander. So, there the two of us were, all alone and that shirt clinging to his skin, his face shiny with sweat. I couldn't resist. As soon as I had an opportunity, I kissed him. I don't know what I expected. I figured he would pull away out of fear or even worse, disgust. But he didn't, he kissed me back. I had been kissed by other young men before, but this wasn't like any kiss I had ever experienced."

"Mother, maybe I've heard just about enough."

"No, trust me, you haven't."

"His kiss was hungry, it was like he *really* wanted me. I don't think most men know how intoxicating that is for a woman, to be wanted like that. Leroy and I spent that entire summer doing nothing but making love to each other every opportunity we got. By the time my parents figured out, I was already pregnant and Leroy's parents sent him away out of fear that he would be imprisoned or maybe even killed.

"I was married off to Richard Bianco shortly thereafter and you were born *prematurely*. There were, of course, rumors, but as far as my mother and father were concerned, Leroy Jackson was never spoken of again. Richard was a bit of a simpleton when we married, but he eventually figured out you were not his son, especially when the two of us never seemed to be able to have a child together. In order to squelch the rumors and probably so he wouldn't have to look at me any longer, my father set your father up in a business that he knew would be successful and that was, of course, far away. That's how we ended up in New York City."

"What are you saying?"

"Son, you know exactly what I'm saying. It would seem that history has repeated itself. You see, you aren't the only person in this family that has an affinity for chocolate. Boy, do I wish I knew where Leroy Jackson was now. I wouldn't care if I had to spend a lifetime in jail, if only I could have one more night with him."

Candace Bianco wasn't finished talking, but Bill was. He hung up the phone and tried to convince himself that all of the women in his life had gone stark raving mad.

CHAPTER TWENTY-NINE

ill got up early in the morning and went looking for the guy with the purple hat on Delancey Street. He tried to push the conversation he'd had earlier with his mother out of his mind and, instead, focused on a plan. He would have to get the passports and the credit cards if there was any hope of saving his family.

The energy on Delancey Street was strange and bore no resemblance to the Delancey Street he remembered as a young boy. The deals now being made were not for discount clothing. Everyone on that street seemed to being looking for some sort of out. There were those who appeared to be in the market for fake identification like himself. If they weren't looking for fake IDs, they were looking for dope. It made perfect sense. If they couldn't escape the poverty and demoralization one way, they would escape it in another. Two blocks away he spotted a man with a purple hat and started to walk quickly to catch up with him.

"Do you know where I can get a passport photo taken?" he asked the man.

"Is it for you?" he asked.

Just as Bill was about to tell him what he needed, he noticed some activity he didn't like. He wondered if it was a set up and as soon as the money exchanged hands he would be carted off to the police.

"You want it or not?" the man asked.

While Bill tried to decide what he should do, he noticed two men walking toward them from the opposite side of the street. If Bill were going to guess, he would have figured them for plain-clothes police detectives. He didn't want to take a chance; at least not yet. Bill quickly walked away, waving his hand at the man in the purple hat.

Before he left the house that day, he gazed at himself for quite some time, trying to decipher if there was any possibility that the story his mother told him was true. He decided it wasn't possible. He was too afraid of what being half-black might mean to analyze the situation objectively. If he had, he would have realized that it made perfect sense that the man he believed to be his father, Richard Bianco, had every reason to resent him.

While Bill was standing silently, looking in the mirror con-templating what it all meant, Traci lay in bed with Caitlin waiting for him to leave. She had her own plans for the day and it didn't involve passports, credit cards or leaving the country; at least not yet. She was going to see her own connection. But the man she was going to see didn't deal in paper; he dealt in guns and lots of them.

Since the world had taken such a drastic turn, Bill had made it a point to always leave more than enough money for Traci in the house, since she obviously couldn't go to any bank or even with-draw money from a cash machine. Usually the money in the house was enough to last her for months but this time she would need most of it. She took two thousand dollars. She hoped she wouldn't need it all but she took that much just in case.

Traci was going in the opposite direction from Bill. She was headed uptown. One thing hadn't changed since the cataclysm started. Harlem had always been the best place to find guns if you needed them, and it still was. They were, of course, difficult to get, but not impossible. All you needed was to have the right connections and that was all Traci had.

"I'm looking for Bo-Bo," she said when she arrived at the Asian-run bodega.

"Bo-Bo in the back," the proprietor informed her.

"What you need, Missy?" Bo-Bo asked, emerging out of nowhere.

"As much as you got."

"You planning on starting a war?"

"Something like that."

"I got plenty, but are you sure you can handle it?"

"I can handle whatever you're selling."

Bo-Bo led her to the back, then laid the firearms out in front of Traci. She picked them up, trying them, checking them.

Bo-Bo wasn't impressed often. But he was now.

It was one of the stories men like him liked to tell to their boys, but these days storytelling was out of the question. He could almost hear himself telling the story, blow by blow. In walks this beautiful, and obviously sophisticated woman, with a little girl on her arm, who looks to be half-white. The woman is obviously well-skilled in the use of firearms. She hands him $1500 and walks out with an arsenal of weapons. Usually, Bo-Bo missed the good old days when he could get so much more money for what he was selling. Even though there was a time when he could have gotten double, or maybe even triple for what he sold her the guns for, this time his disappointment was minimal. He might not be able to tell the story now. But he was hopeful that one day he might be able to tell it. Until then, he would keep it tucked away and draw upon it when he needed an excuse to smile.

"Good-bye, Bo-Bo," Caitlin said as they were leaving.

Bo-Bo made a mental note not to leave those last words spoken by the little girl, as her and her mother left, out of the story.

"Bye, little lady."

Traci also purchased silencers from Bo-Bo and used them while she practiced in the basement.

As soon as she heard Bill arrive, she hid the guns and came upstairs.

"What were you doing down there?" Bill asked.

"Securing a place to hide," she lied.

Suddenly Traci realized it was not a horrible idea. It would make a perfect fortress.

Bill couldn't stand to think of his wife and his daughter being forced to find a place to hide in their own home. It was bordering on barbaric. "You won't have to do that. I'm going to get us some passports and credit cards and we're getting out of here."

"Yeah. Where are we going to go?"

"I was thinking Italy."

"Italy, really? You've got to be kidding me. There is no way the three of us are going to get anywhere near Italy from here. Or have you forgotten the numeric equation? One white man, plus one black woman, plus one multiracial child equals no entry. I can't even ride the subway with Caitlin and you're suggesting that we'll be able to get on an airplane and just fly out of the country. I could have a passport that attests to the fact that I'm The Queen of England, complete with matching photo, and I'd still never be able to get out of the United States; especially not with Caitlin, and I will not go anywhere without my daughter."

Bill couldn't help but recognize that the events that had transpired over the years had hardened Traci. She wasn't the same sweet, and often naïve, young woman he had married. He didn't think she would ever be the same again.

"Don't we at least owe it to ourselves to try?"

"You can try, but Caitlin and I are staying here."

"What are you saying, Traci? We belong together."

"Do we really? All I've heard since we got together is how we shouldn't be together. First your mother tried to block our relationship, then the government. There comes a time when you have to recognize that it may be the cosmo's way of telling you something."

For weeks Bill tried to get passports, to no avail. And, for weeks Traci continued to prepare for a call to arms. Bill noticed that she was constantly writing in a small notebook but never pressed her to explain. Instead, he tried to see things from her perspective and realized Traci was probably right. Even if he did get the passports, chances were slim to none that they'd be able to do anything with them. He decided that his place was there with his girls in the home they had built.

Bill went down to the basement. Finally convinced that Traci was probably making more sense than he gave her credit for and deciding he would make the basement as comfortable as possible, just in case they did need to hide there, he went in the basement to see what he could do with it. He was exploring all the nooks and crannies when he uncovered Traci's stash of weapons. He wondered what the small arsenal could possibly be for. Instead of acting on his first instinct and confronting her as soon as she returned him, he decided he would wait and the next time she left home, instead of paying someone, as he had done in the past, he would follow Traci himself and see where she went. It was less than twenty-four hours later when he had his chance.

Donning her usual makeup, Traci, prepared both herself and Caitlin, complete with foundation, hoodies and a large bag.

Bill was surprised at how easy it was to infiltrate the group and watched silently from the back, wearing the same foundation Traci and Caitlin often wore, only in a dark brown shade. He even remembered to apply it to his hands as well.

Bill looked carefully around the room, curious as to whom the leader was. That's when Traci rose, walked to the podium and began to speak.

"Many of you may be asking yourselves, what can I do?" she shouted. "Well, the next time you find yourself asking that question, respond with *I am powerful beyond words*. I will fight for my release and the release of my children. I will no longer be a slave. I will rise up, I will hold a knife in one hand and a gun in the other, if I have to, but I will be victorious. I will free myself. I will bring those that oppress me down!"

Everyone in the room cheered, including Caitlin. Bill couldn't understand it, but instead of being angry with her he was actually proud. It would appear that his wife was a force to be reckoned with.

Bill was shocked when Traci's ex-boyfriend, Bryan, joined her on the platform. Bill had heard rumors that Bryan was dead. Yet, there he was with Traci. Suddenly Bill was boiling mad. Wherein, he was first concerned about what kind of a mess she was wrapped up in and then proud of her strength, now he was pissed off and sure that she was having an affair.

Then it dawned on him. His four-year-old daughter was standing with the others, a gun in her hand as well. When Bryan hoisted Caitlin onto his shoulders and she began giggling, it was more than Bill could stand. It was as though he had been replaced and it was sick. He realized that if he did anything to alert the others that he was there they would probably tear him limb from limb.

That night he left anonymously with the crowd and watched as they piled into cars and trucks and drove. They all went in different directions. He got in his own car and followed Traci and Caitlin.

"Always be prepared," Traci said.

"I know, Mommy. I'm prepared."

"What do you aim for?"

"The heart or the head."

"Good girl. What else, pumpkin?"

"I only shoot on your order."

"Exactly. Ready?"

"Ready?"

Traci, Caitlin and two other cars full of people burst through someone's home, guns drawn and began shooting. Bill recognized the place as the home of a local Republican politician who had been one of the strongest advocates of racial separation. He heard at least ten shots fired and was afraid for Caitlin. He couldn't imagine what Traci was thinking, involving Caitlin in such mayhem.

When Traci and Caitlin returned home, they behaved as though they had done nothing more interesting than going for a walk.

Bill was sitting in the living room waiting for them.

"Hi, Daddy."

"Hello, sweet pea. Go to your room and get ready for bed."

"But Daddy, it's early and I'm hungry."

"You hear that? Your four-year-old daughter said she's hungry," he said to Traci when Caitlin was out of earshot. "Why hasn't she eaten yet? I followed you tonight, Traci. I know what you've been doing."

"How much did you see?"

"Enough."

"Then you know that I have no intention of stopping. So do your worst."

"Did Caitlin fire any of those shots I heard tonight?"

"No, not tonight."

"Does that mean she has before?"

"Not often, but if the situation calls for it she is fully prepared to fight as well as anyone else in our group. I was sure to train her well."

"Are you even listening to yourself? She's a four-year-old girl. You have her out killing people."

"We don't kill people. We protect our rights. Our right to bear arms, our right to justice, tranquility, welfare and liberty, just like it says in the Constitution. You said you followed us. Did you know that the family that lived in the house we visited tonight was keeping slaves like they were living in the seventeen hundreds? People are starving out here, and people like that Senator and his wife were capitalizing at every turn.

"Well, they're not anymore. When I saw those kids living under those conditions, I was glad I had come. No human being deserves to live like a dog. That family of four sleeps in the garage. They have no real beds to speak of. When it's cold, there is no heat and when it's hot, no air conditioning. The mother told me that her and her family work anywhere from ten to twenty hours a day."

"Traci, you need help."

"Have you forgotten, people like me are unworthy of help? When your mother dies, she'll have a funeral fit for a queen. My brother's body was probably tossed out like yesterday's garbage. This world is such that I couldn't even go and get my brother's body and give him a proper burial.

"There's no closure for me. My brother and I were always very close and then suddenly one day he was gone. That image of him swinging from that tree will be burned into my memory forever. Not only his face, beaten until he looked like ground beef, but all the faces. Did you *really* look at those pictures? Those people were somebody's father, somebody's brother, somebody's husband or lover. Their lives were treated like they were meaningless. Once again, black people are being reminded that we are not considered equals. I will not allow my child to live in a world where she can't be considered an equal. I will fight until my last breath because that is what I'm supposed to do."

CHAPTER THIRTY

Bill felt powerless. Traci was doing whatever she wanted and with his daughter always in tow. Both she and Caitlin had stopped sleeping in their bedrooms at night and only used the other rooms in the house during the day. At night Traci took Caitlin out with her and killed people. They were still in the same position they had been in for the last two years so Bill found it hard to reconcile what she was doing as right. Whenever he tried to talk to her about it, she spouted off something about the Constitution or different laws that were enacted, both past and present. Bill was now fully convinced that Traci was quite insane.

It wasn't until he heard her speak to people other than himself that he realized she didn't seem quite so insane when dealing with others. There was something about her interactions with him that caused a break in her thinking. He knew that now and wondered if he should simply leave. Whenever he had that thought, he thought of Caitlin and understood he couldn't leave.

"Daddy, look what I drew. It's a picture of you and me and Mommy."

Bill was struck by the fact that in the picture they were all the same color. He wondered if that had anything to do with the makeup her and her mother so often wore, in order to go unnoticed. On top of the picture was the word *revolution*."

"Who wrote that?" Bill asked.

"I did, Daddy."

"No, really, Caitlin. Who wrote it?"

"She did write it," Traci explained.

"She can't even spell. How can she write a word like revolution?"

"Caitlin can spell. She knows many words. Or, have you forgotten that once upon a time her mother was a teacher? In fact, Caitlin is actually a very smart little girl and I'm not just saying that because she's my daughter.

"She is learning French, her addition and multiplication tables and she is an excellent speller. It's a shame she can't go to school like other kids but I am working every day to ensure that one day she will."

"You mean by killing people?"

"Absolutely. It was Malcolm X that said it first; by any means necessary. This is our means. We tried to do things the non-violent way and that accomplished nothing. Now, we're doing things the violent way. Maybe if we kill enough people someone will get the message and make some changes. I had to lose half of my family and for what. For what? So that some fat cat somewhere could enjoy some misplaced sense of superiority. I'm done with losing people. I am going to do everything within my power to ensure that no one else is lost due to someone else's cruelty."

"And you think you can accomplish that by killing the people that you think deserve to die?"

"Hell yeah."

"And what happens when you show up at someone's house one night and they've got a gun or a knife and are ready to shoot, or cut your throat or Caitlin's?"

"Then we will have died for a good cause."

"It's fine to make that decision for yourself but what right do you have to make that decision for our daughter?"

"I have *every* right. I'm her mother."

"What about me? Don't I have any rights?"

"You lost your rights the moment you stopped fighting for us."

"Stop this now and I'll fight for you. I'll do anything you say."

"Do you mean it? Then the next time we go out, go with us."

"That's not what I mean, Traci, and you know it's not."

"Then I guess you aren't ready to fight for us like you said. Or, do anything I say."

"Okay, how about this? How about I stay home with Caitlin and you go out and do what you feel you must do?"

"What do you think, I'm stupid? I go out and come back to find both you and my daughter gone. Besides, Caitlin needs to learn how to survive in the world she was born into. We did it. We navigated the waters of what was handed to us. She wasn't born into our world. She was born into her own and if she doesn't learn how to make it work for her, and early, she'll never survive."

"I'm afraid she's not going to survive living your way," Bill said. "I wouldn't do that to Caitlin. I know how much you mean to her."

"Really?"

"Yes, really."

"So, I go out and take care of business and you and Caitlin are waiting here for me when I return?"

"Exactly."

"It would be a lot easier on my own and Caitlin is now fully trained. It's not like anyone can take that knowledge away from her. I agree. I want Caitlin to be able to live to fight another day and although she has held her own quite well, she is still too young. The only reason I was training her was because I didn't know what to do with her. It's not like I could ring up a babysitter for the night. There are now so many traitors within the COC that none of us knows who to trust. I did take care of that Preston

Chambers, though. I was convinced that he was the one that turned my brother in and Mr. Chambers paid dearly for that little mistake."

Each subsequent night that followed, Traci was out doing exactly what she told Bill she would do. She was always concerned that one night she would return to find the house empty but each night Caitlin was sleeping peacefully in her bed and Bill was either in the bedroom or living room waiting.

"Traci, how long can you continue doing this? Aren't you tired?"

"Of course I'm tired. I've been tired for quite some time, but that means nothing. I was tired before I even picked up a gun. Now, at least, I feel like I'm doing something."

"The rules are still in full force and effect. We are still prisoners here."

"Correction, Caitlin and I are still prisoners here. You can leave anytime you like."

As if in response to what Traci said the phone suddenly rang. Bill saw his mother's number on the Caller ID and picked it up.

"They know," his mother said.

"They know what?" Bill asked.

"They know about you." she said.

CHAPTER THIRTY-ONE

*T*raci only heard Bill's end of the conversation and assumed that they were coming for her and Caitlin. She had seen numerous cases like this. Nothing would happen to Bill. They typically held the white party overnight, pretty much to put a scare into them and make them an example for anyone else that considered breaking the actively enforced law. But eventually they were let go. What happened to the black person and the offspring was another story altogether. Some of the stories were horrible.

Traci quickly gathered up Caitlin and hurried to the basement. Bill had built out a separate and very small area that was undetectable and could safely hide both Traci and Caitlin together, quite well. All night Traci waited for them to come but they never did.

Bill had no intention of sharing with Traci the information he had just learned. Now it wasn't just her and Caitlin that were in danger, it was him as well.

"But if they know that I'm half-black, then isn't this a good thing?" he continued, after Traci left. "Doesn't that mean my marriage to Traci isn't unlawful at all."

"Sadly, that is not what it means. You are still half-white and your marriage is still considered just as unlawful as if both your parents were white."

"How on earth did they find out?"

"It was all my fault and I'm going to do everything in my power to protect you and your family. I'm a foolish old woman. I've been so lonely since you got married and that night I called you and told you about your real father, I couldn't get Leroy out of my mind, so I went in search of him. I found him, by the way, and he would like to see you. Well, after locating him, the family that I have working for me told the authorities and exchanged the information they had for money and the chance to leave here."

"What now?"

"I was contacted by a detective at the Fifty-First Precinct. He suggested you turn yourself in."

"Let me have his number."

"You're not actually considering turning yourself in, are you?"

"Give me a little time. I'll figure something out. This is my fault. I'm going to do something to help you. There has to be something."

"Mom, if there was something, don't you think either Traci or I would have figured it out by now?"

In fact, Bill had figured something out. It might not have been the most morally sound thing he had ever done, but he was desperate. While he considered what he was going to say to Traci, he looked at the phone number for the detective that he had written down. He decided he would call while Caitlin and Traci were still in the basement. It was morning and they would both be coming out of the basement soon to eat breakfast.

"Hello, may I speak to Detective Warren?"

"Who is calling?"

"This is Bill Bianco. I understand there may be a warrant out for my arrest."

"Not yet, Mr. Bianco, but one may be issued, and soon."

"What do I need to do?"

"Just come in and talk with me. We'll figure something out."

Bill left the house before Traci and Caitlin left the basement and went to the precinct.

"I'm here to see Detective Warren," he announced at the front desk.

"Warren, there's someone here to see you. What did you say your name was?"

"Bill Bianco."

"A Mr. Bianco is here to see you."

A few seconds later, Detective Warren appeared from around a wall. "Mr. Bianco, let me explain to you something that has become a bit of a sticky situation."

"Absolutely."

"Your wife or should I say your ex-wife, based on reports I've received?"

"Ex-wife."

"Your ex-wife is involved in a very militant organization called The C.O.C. Until recently the group was little more than a slight annoyance. However, recently this same organization has become increasingly violent. They have killed and wounded countless city officials and they have to be stopped. There has been an ongoing investigation and it would appear that these murders started right about the time your brother-in-law, one Darren Sanders, died in Mississippi. We believe that your ex-wife, in some quest for vengeance, has taken up her brother's fight in quite an aggressive fashion and she is indeed chiefly responsible for these murders. I know she is not working alone and that there are other members of the group working with her. But, it is my belief that Ms. Sanders is the leader."

Bill sat in silence, not uttering a word and allowing it all to sink in.

"You wouldn't happen to know anything about this, would you, Mr. Bianco?"

"What if I do?"

"If you do, it would be to your advantage to tell us everything you know."

"Then what?" Bill asked.

"Then, if everything you say checks out, you walk out of here a free man."

"It all sounds so easy."

"That's because it is. It's very easy. All we want is her and whoever she's been committing these murders with. Unless you've been helping her, we have no desire to cause any problems for you."

Just as Bill was about to speak, his mother entered the precinct.

"My son has a right to an attorney."

"Mr. Bianco is not under arrest."

"Then why is he here?"

"He came of his own accord."

"Bill?"

"Mother, it's fine."

"If my son is not under arrest, then that means I can speak to him in private if I'd like."

"Feel free," the detective said.

Candace Bianco took her son off to the side to try and figure out what was on his mind. "Why would you come here, unless..." She gazed into his eyes. "Son, no. That's not you. Don't tell me you've come here to turn Traci and Caitlin in."

"No, of course not. I have a plan, but your presence here is not helping matters any."

"Just think about whatever it is you're planning to do before you do it. You wouldn't want to do something you can't take back."

"I understand," he assured his mother.

Candace left the precinct, but not before making a point of rolling her eyes at the detective who was questioning her son.

"Wow, she's something else, huh?"

"That's my mother. What can I say?"

"So, before she walked in, you were saying."

"I know everything there is to know about Traci. What is it that you want to know?"

"Well, first of all, is she or isn't she a killer?"

"I believe the C.O.C. has been taking it upon themselves to kill some people they consider undesirables."

"And were any of those people, to your knowledge, city officials?"

"I believe so."

"You know we are going to need you to put all of this in writing?"

"Yes. I'd also like something in writing."

"What's that?"

"What you said earlier; that I can walk out of here a free man."

"Absolutely. We'll put something together now."

The police had Bill write out a statement and sign it. In return, they provided him with papers stating that he would not be punished for his ethnic makeup or his marriage to Traci Sanders.

By the time Bill got outside, the paper he had received from the detective in hand, he was wracked with guilt already, as his mother had predicted. He resolved to deal with his guilt, however, and do his best to move on. After all, he was still a young man and had no desire to spend the rest of his days in prison. His mother may have attempted to make him believe that he wouldn't be in prison for long, but any length of time would have been too much and what did she know. He could have been in there longer than she believed. Now he would be free. Traci and his daughter would not be if he couldn't get them out in time but, according to Traci, they weren't free anyway, so at this point it was little more than a matter of geography.

By the time Bill returned home, Traci and Caitlin were both out of the basement, and surprisingly Traci was in their bedroom. It had been quite some time since she had spent any time there. She was looking at some newspapers he knew she hid under a floor-board in the closet.

"What you got there?" Bill asked.

"Nothing," Traci lied.

"You and I both know that's not the truth. You know what would happen if that was found?"

"Yeah, I know, the same thing that will happen if I'm found. Who would have thought that one day I'd be a prisoner in my own home? I can't leave and I can't stay. Ironic, isn't it?"

"It's only temporary. I'm making plans. We're going to get out. We're going to get out together."

Traci knew exactly what that meant. For months Bill had tried everything he could to get passports for Traci and Caitlin and when he realized that might not work even if he did secure a password, he realized he would have to find a way to escape from the U.S. with or without a passport. The question Traci kept asking him was where? The U.S. had not been the only country affected. For quite some time they believed the only alternative they had was to somehow make it to Germany, where her brother and sister-in-law were. Unfortunately, over time it had become apparent that even Germany was a dangerous gamble.

Bill observed the forlorn look on Traci's face and searched for the words to fill her with some small remnant of hope.

"There has to be somewhere we can go. The entire world can't be affected by this madness. There's always been some other place to go, even in light of the greatest despair."

The frightening and intrusive presence of what sounded like a battering ram pounding against their front door signaled the realization that, for Traci and Bill Bianco, time had run out.

Bill never expected them to arrive so quickly. He fully believed that he at least had twenty-four hours. He had his papers. He was going to warn Traci and she would take the passports he had gotten for both her and Caitlin and they could go to Mexico. Many of the people that were escaping persecution were going to Mexico when they realized going to Europe was impossible and Mexico was easy and no one there asked any questions. But now there was no time.

Several officers rushed in, guns drawn, and ordered both Traci and Bill to the ground. Bill realized he could still help Traci and Caitlin from the outside. He had the papers the detectives had signed earlier.

"Get down, now! Down! Down!"

Traci was facedown on the ground while Bill was waving the papers in his hand.

"I'm not going to tell you again. One more time and we shoot."

"Bill, get down," Traci yelled. She was thinking of Caitlin nearby and fearful the officer's shots might hit their daughter. "Bill, honey, please, just do what they say," she begged him.

"But I have these papers! I have papers!" he said.

Traci wondered what papers he was talking about.

One of the officers grabbed the papers out of Bill's hand and read them.

"According to this, the detective allowed you to walk out of the precinct with your sworn testimony. It says nothing about future arrests."

"Bill, what is he talking about? What sworn testimony?" she asked.

"According to this statement, your wonderful little hubby swore to the fact that he witnessed you murder several people. Quite the little knight-in-shining-armor, ain't he?"

"What are they saying, Bill? Tell me you didn't. Please God! Tell me you didn't?" When he did not respond, she continued, "What kind of a man are you? You would turn in your wife and your child; and for what? What was it for, Bill? Tell me. It couldn't have been for money. Between you and your mother, you've got plenty of that. Why did you do it?"

"Sometimes people are too stubborn to save themselves. So, does that mean I should perish because you wouldn't fucking listen? I was desperate. Besides, I had a plan. I was going to get here in enough time to help you and Caitlin escape."

"Brilliant plan. And, this isn't about me. It's about our daughter; our flesh and blood. You would rather see her suffer than to be a man."

"I am a man!"

"You're not a man. My brother was a man. Bryan is a man. You're just some little boy still stuck behind his mommy's apron string."

Bill slapped Traci, hard, across the face.

The officers did nothing to stop him.

"Daddy, don't do that. You hurt Mommy. Don't hit her."

Caitlin came running toward her father.

"One of you needs to tell the little girl to sit down."

"Caitlin, honey, please sit down. Sit down for Mommy, okay?"

"Is that *the* okay, Mommy? Is it?"

Caitlin Bianco was a perfect shot. With a small handgun, she fired twice, hitting two officers right in the forehead. It caught the remaining officers off-guard long enough to allow Traci to pull her weapon from the front of her waistband, jump up and begin firing.

"Get down, Caitlin! Get down now!"

Caitlin always obeyed her mother without question and was on the floor quickly.

With all of the officers killed, Bill finally got up off the floor.
One of the officer's guns was in his hand.

"The only way I'm getting out of this without life in prison is if
you're dead. I've got these papers, clearing me. It was you they
were looking for all along. I could be a hero. You killed the officers
and then I killed you."

"What about our daughter, Bill? Do you have a plan for her?
What about Caitlin?"

Traci and Bill were both pointing guns at each other. With
Bill's other hand he was vigorously massaging his temples.

"Not so clean, huh? Not so easy to kill an innocent child, is it;
especially your own child? I can't believe there was a time when I
loved you so much. It's true what they say, a person's true character
comes out when faced with dire circumstances."

"It didn't have to be this way, Traci. You just wouldn't let up. I
kept begging you to wait it out, to not push so hard. But, you just
couldn't do it. You needed things to change overnight. I kept trying
to tell you, it didn't get that way overnight and it wasn't going to
suddenly be resolved overnight. But no, you kept right on pushing
and pushing and pushing. What the fuck is wrong with you? Things
could have been good for us, even under the worst of circumstances.
I would have taken care of you and Caitlin forever."

"Yeah, I see how you've *taken care* of us."

"Stop twisting my words around. Caitlin, come here, baby. Come
to Daddy."

"Okay, Daddy. What's wrong? You don't like me and Mommy
using guns?"

"No, sweetheart. I don't like you and Mommy using guns.
Guns are bad."

"But Daddy, you have a gun and you're pointing it at Mommy.
That's not nice. Mommy is one of the good guys."

"What about Daddy, precious? Is Daddy one of the good guys?" Bill asked.

"Yes, Daddy."

The first shot caught Bill Bianco in the chest and the second went straight through his temple. Traci was happy it hadn't been Caitlin that fired. That would have been a painful memory she would have been forced to carry with her the rest of her life.

Instead, Traci had taken care of it. Bill would have killed both her and Caitlin without blinking so much as an eye. Even if he didn't kill them, he would be a liability to them. He would have never stopped believing that they were meant to be and he would have never stopped believing that his way was the right way. His eyes were open and if it wasn't for the bullet hole through his head, she might have believed he was still alive. She remembered the first time she had seen those beautiful eyes and wondered how something she thought was so right could go so wrong so quickly.

She looked around the home she once thought was so beautiful. Now it seemed little more than a prison. Just as she tried to figure out what her next move should be and where she should go, Bryan and several other members of the C.O.C. were standing at her door.

"What, did you think we didn't know? The C.O.C. knows all and sees all. And, don't you forget it," Bryan said solemnly.

"Next time, it would be nice if you guys *saw* things just a bit sooner. I'm sweating bullets here."

"So where to next?" Bryan asked. "A tropical island or something even more exotic? Actually, I have something even better in mind. It's something I think you're going to like."

By morning they were at a lovely little remote village called

Emiliano Zapata. Waiting to greet them were her brother, Sebastian, and his wife, Angelika, and someone Traci never thought she'd ever see again, her best friend, mentor and confidante, Sandra Piper.

"What took you so long?" Sandra asked Traci.

"I had a few stops I had to make along the way."

EPILOGUE

A beautiful, long-legged blonde stands out amongst a sea of Mexicans. She is popular amongst the natives and is, in some respects, a native herself. Despite her obvious femininity, her strong gait is anything but feminine. She takes deliberate strides toward a group of men playing cards.

"Deal me in."

"No, senorita. None of the men will play if you play."

"Chicken shits!"

Strapped to her upper leg is a firearm. There is another at her ankle and at her bodice is a switchblade.

"Senorita, why do you play cards with the men? You need a husband. You should get married and have lots of babies."

"Tino, now you sound like my mother. I don't want to get married. There are far more important things for a woman to do in this world, then play second to a man.

An attractive black woman in her fifties joins them. "It's my own fault, Tino. I let her play with guns and knives too much when she was a little girl. Now, she thinks she's a boy."

"I do not!"

"You certainly walk like a boy. And, oh my goodness, shut your legs. You certainly sit like a boy. You're not a lesbian, are you? It's okay if you are. My best friend is a lesbian and my brother was homosexual. I miss that fool. Your Uncle Darren could make me want to kill him one minute and shower him with kisses in the next. I wish you remembered him. He would have been floored by you. Darren was gay, but there was one thing he adored and that was beautiful women."

"Do you really think I'm beautiful?"

"Girl, go on over there and look in that mirror." Her sandy blonde lion's main spread out over head; her skin was tan from years of living in Mexico, and she had the kind of body that comes from being twenty-one and dynamite.

Traci Sanders sat, fanning herself.

"You okay, Mom?" Caitlin asked.

"I'm fine, baby. I'm so tired of missing people. You know, there was a time long ago, before I was even born, when the average life expectancy was thirty-five. But, eventually that evolved into a much higher number. It wasn't unheard of for people to live until eighty-five or even ninety-years old. Our life expectancy seems to be getting shorter once again. I've said good-bye to so many people, I'm starting to feel like a dinosaur—your father, Darren, my mother, now Bryan. You may not remember because you were so young, but Bryan was the one who brought us here. We had our problems in the early years, but our time here in Mexico together was paradise. I'm going to miss him. Who would have thought that after all the years of him and I fighting side by side he would die of an illness like cancer?"

Caitlin smiled. "He told me he wanted to die in battle, not in no hospital bed. Uncle Bryan was a bad-ass!"

"What do you want for your birthday, Ms. Caitlin?"

"I already have everything I need."

"Not something you need. There must be something you want. I already have a surprise coming for you, but I want to get you something else."

"I want to try out that new gun Aunty Sandra gave me for my birthday. I'll be back."

"Ah, shoot. My surprise is early," Traci said.

She looked up to find her guests had arrived. Walking in front was a tall, muscular gent with beautiful red hair and next to him was a distinguished-looking older man.

"You still hiding out here in this tiny little village? You do know things are getting better each day in New York, and all over the country, thanks to you. We elected our very first black female President of the United States. She is just as impressive as her father ever was. Thank goodness for the C.O.C. They protected her from harm, even after the President, her mother and sister were both killed. Now, she can carry on her father's legacy. The economy is still in a mess of trouble, but I have every confidence that things will be looking up soon. So where is the little lady?"

"That *little lady* as you call her is twenty-one years old today and she ain't so little."

Caitlin came bouncing back and recognized Jacob immediately. She almost jumped out of her skin. "Jacob!"

"Caitlin Bianco. Wow! Wow!"

Traci whispered in her daughter's ear. "See, I told you you're beautiful. Now let's get this party started! Caitlin Bianco, would you please put those guns away?"

"Fiesta!" Tino yelled.

ABOUT THE AUTHOR

Michelle Janine Robinson is the author of the Zane Presents novel *Serial Typical* (July 2012), *More Than Meets The Eye* (June 2011) and *Color Me Grey* (June 2010). All titles were published by Simon & Schuster/Strebor Books. Michelle's short story contribution *"The Quiet Room"* was a featured story in the *New York Times* bestseller *Succulent: Chocolate Flava II*. She has contributed to several other anthologies, including *Caramel Flava, Honey Flava, Purple Panties* and *Tasting Him*. In 2009 *Tasting Him* won the IPPY (Independent Publisher) Award for Erotica. Urban Reviews listed Michelle's debut novel, *Color Me Grey*, as one of the best reviewed books on UrbanReviewsOnline.com for 2010. In February 2011 Michelle was voted *Writers POV Magazine's* Annual Winter Writing Contest Winner of the Year and in March 2011 Michelle was voted a National Black Book Festival finalist for Best New Author of the Year. Michelle is a native New Yorker and the mother of identical twins. You can also find Michelle at www.facebook.com/michelle.j.robinson, www.myspace.com/justef or follow Michelle at www.twitter.com/MJanineRobinson.

CHAPTER ONE

Damita was happier today than she had ever been in her entire life. She was marrying her soul mate; the man she would spend the rest of her life with. Neal was a successful architect and she was an investment banker. They had been dating for little more than a year when he popped the question at the restaurant where they had their first date, The Sea Grill, at Rockefeller Center. He even got down on one knee to propose in front of a restaurant full of people. It just didn't get much better than that. The only thing that would have made this a happier occasion is if her friends and family were as elated as she was. Somehow, as charming as Neal was, he had gotten off on the wrong foot with both her mother and her girlfriends. They thought he was pompous and a bit of a narcissist. But, they didn't know him like she knew him. He was gentle and kind and he cared for her, unlike anyone else ever had. He was all she ever wanted; all she ever needed. And, he was hers.

On her wedding day Damita's mother stood in the doorway watching her.

"You are absolutely beautiful."

"Oh Mama, you startled me."

"You know what your grandmother used to say: *Why you jumpin' like that? You must not be livin' right*. Or, maybe it's not *you* that's not livin' right?"

"Mama, you promised you would behave yourself today."

"Yeah, yeah, yeah, I know. But, I wouldn't be your mother if I didn't ask you one more time whether you're sure this is what you want to do?"

"I'm 110% sure."

"Mr. Brooks Brothers is outside barking orders to everybody. I swear I don't believe I've ever seen a man take that much interest in a wedding in my entire life. He's surveyed everything, including the doggone flowers. It just ain't natural."

"You should be happy he's taking an interest. He's only doing it because he loves me and he wants me to have the best wedding day ever."

"Are you sure it's not because he's controlling as hell and he's paying for the wedding, so he wants to make sure he gets exactly what he paid for?"

"So, what's wrong with that? Neal didn't get where he is by squandering his money. It's one of the things I love about him. I feel safe with him; like I can count on a secure future."

"Security comes from within baby, not from a man or from money."

Damita was so wrapped up in her impending nuptials she couldn't be bothered to truly pay attention to the importance of what her mother was saying.

"Yes, Mama, I know. I know. But, you don't have to keep telling me these things. You and Daddy raised me to be a strong, independent young woman. Just because I've fallen in love, doesn't mean I've forgotten everything you both taught me."

"It's just your choice of words, Damita; words like *security* and *fallen* in love. Words like that have always been red flags for me when it comes to relationships. Somehow the world has embraced the theory that love is something you fall into. That's not love. That's a temporary distraction and once the distraction is gone, what's left?"

"I'm not you Mom. You and Daddy were married for forty-two years before he died. Things have changed quite a bit since the days when you got married."

"I know, I'm a dinosaur, but I'm not so much of a dinosaur that I don't see you possibly giving up the better part of what makes you, you."

"I promise you that will never happen."

"I hope not."

"This is supposed to be a happy occasion. I want you to walk with me down the aisle and I want you to be happy for me, okay? Neal is everything I've always wanted in a man. I've got a great job. I'm healthy—and dare I say—not unattractive, and I've got this perfect man so in love with me. Mama, I'm sitting on top of the world."

"Just don't forget that you are still ALL of those things, with or without a man."

"I won't."

Her mother didn't want to point out her use of one of those red flag words, *perfect*. Instead, she decided to drop the subject.

The minister's secretary opened the door.

"Are you ready?" she asked.

"Yes, I am," Damita responded emphatically.

Her mother wanted to be excited for her; could see how happy her daughter was. But, Karen knew within every fiber of her being that Neal was not the right man for her daughter. But, oftentimes, the most any parent could do was tread softly in explaining their viewpoint. There were certain things that your children had to learn on their own. She just hoped the lesson wouldn't come with too great a cost. But, she knew, no matter what, she would be there to cushion her daughter if she fell.

The wedding ceremony complete, the reception was in full effect and everyone seemed to be enjoying themselves, when Damita saw Neal heading toward her with what appeared to be a scowl on his face.

"What is he doing here?" Neal asked.

"Who, baby?"

"You know exactly who. What is your ex doing here?"

"We've been married all of an hour and you're jealous already," Damita teased.

"Damita, I'm not joking. Who invited him?"

"My mom...and me," she added, not wanting Neal to resent her mother.

"I figured it was your mother. All I want to know is why she despises me so much. I have been nothing but cordial and respectful to the woman.

Yet, she likes that nobody better than she does her own son-in-law."

"Brandon is like family. My whole family...and I have known Brandon since we were both in kindergarten together."

"How would you feel if I invited one of my old girlfriends to our wedding? You wouldn't like it very much, would you?"

"Okay, I understand. I'm sorry. I probably should have asked you first. I just didn't think it would be that big a deal."

"It's a big fucking deal!"

It was the first time Damita had heard Neal curse or even raise his voice. It was something she hoped she wouldn't hear often.

The wedding reception continued without event. Damita tried her best to steer Brandon clear of Neal and with the hundred or so guests in attendance, her task wasn't too difficult. She considered enlisting the aid of her best friend, Carmella, but she knew that would mean explaining why. And, the last thing she wanted to do was lend credence to everyone's doubts about her new husband, especially Carmella.

"Girl, you okay?"

"I'm good. I guess I'm just a little tired."

"I knew it! That's why your ass got married. You're pregnant, aren't you?"

"No, I'm not pregnant. But, I do plan on trying as soon as possible. After all, I'm 35 years old. I'm not getting any younger and that damned clock is getting louder and louder with each birthday."

"That's not why you got married, is it? Because of your biological clock?"

"No, Carmella, I married Neal because I absolutely, positively adore him."

"I'm sorry, girl, I just don't see it."

Carmella glanced over at Neal, adjusting his tie so that it was perfectly straight. She didn't mention it to Damita at that moment, but it occurred to her that he had all the earmarks of a serial killer, with all that fidgeting and adjusting—the perfection. Then, as if on cue, he did what he always did, stared directly at Damita. Damita and Neal had been dating for over a year, but from the very first time she met him, Carmella always noticed how he never, ever allowed Damita to get too far away from his birds-eyeview. Damita thought it was endearing. Carmella thought it was just plain ole creepy. She had known her share of obsessive, controlling men. And, in her experience, relationships with men such as Neal, always ended badly.

As Carmella watched Neal watching Damita, she sensed something different in him. There was a certain air of cockiness that was somehow more intense than it had been before. That's when it occurred to Carmella what it was. He had won *the prize*. He no longer had to play the role for Damita's family or friends. She was now his wife and there was nothing any of them could do about it.

As Carmella and Neal both eye-balled one another, neither of them willing to admit defeat, Brandon joined Carmella and Damita on the other side of the room.

He grabbed both Carmella and Damita around the neck simultaneously, hugging them to him.

"So I guess that leaves you, Carmella. This one here has broken my heart and married someone else, so I guess I'll have to marry you, Carmella."

"Uh-uh, I'm no one's booby prize."

"Naw, naw, it's not like that. All these years I've been biding my time, getting cozy with Damita in order to get to her hot, Latina friend."

"I know that's right," Carmella agreed.

Although Carmella didn't think Damita, nor anyone else, noticed, Neal's response to Brandon's presence was unmistakable. He was clearly steaming with anger.